I0599842

The Writhing, Verdant End

Corey Farrenkopf, Tiffany Morris, and Eric Raglin

Cursed Morsels Press

Contents

Notice of Content Warnings

Many of these stories deal with intense subject matter. Content warnings are available at the back of the book.

The Final Sight
by Corey Farrenkopf

1. Merek

They sit with binoculars raised, concave lenses staring across the chasm to the green expanses beyond, verdant trees in full bloom, bird song glimpsed, but never heard. Some haven't moved in days. Some in weeks. The stench is awful. The rusting beach chairs crumble beneath their reclined forms, holdovers from ages past, when there were actually beaches. Their stare never drifts down to what seethes in the pit, what keeps them from spanning the distance to inhabit that other realm of evergreen splendor. There's a reason the Watchers don't leave their seats. There's a reason they have accepted the lives they've inherited. The withering. The supposed glory of the final sight. The realm after this realm.

It is said that the last sight you see upon death, that will be the space your mind inhabits for the rest of eternity, the promised heaven you could never step foot in while your lungs drew breath. That is why half of the chairs are filled with the dead, heads lulling, binoculars stolen by the next generation of devotees.

But we will not be like them.

We will not press those lenses to our eyes.

The chasm drops away just beyond the Watcher's boots, hundreds of feet down, incline steep, almost unscalable. I still don't know how those creatures survive the fall. The jagged rocks. The sudden stop. But there they are, the warped amalgams of deer and gull and bear and coyote and shrew. If the Watchers were to tilt their binoculars down, they'd view the broiling mass, bodies welded together, muscle and sinew stitched through chemical exposure and drinking water residue, all those compounds that should never have existed in the soil, in the air, flesh folding into flesh. They amble and shiver like leaves in the wind, life fled from eyes, yet still somehow present in their limbs. They tear at those who try to make the crossing, those that descend the lone ladder to the base of the gorge, to where our neighbors had corralled the monstrosities for generations, never realizing they were sealing off their one escape route, their one chance to avoid the same end.

For a time, the gathering horde hadn't been more concerning than everything else in our blood-blighted lives. Food was scarce. Drinking water the same. So we worried about those immediate things ... and other things. The regional territorial wars. The rise and fall of cul-de-sac fiefdoms. The blood mold. The night vanishers. The cannibal cults. The cannibal religions.

The so-called cannibal deities. The amalgams were low on our priority list. Low until more human shapes started to amble about the gorge. No one noticed their warped neighbors descend the ladder, the way growths twisted arms, their necks, the muscles in their face. The way a frog might meld with the skin on a leg, how a horse might drag them forth as a forever rider, a haunted centaur grafted at the wrong angle. But there was no doubt, the amalgams called to other amalgams, drawn like magnets to cursed metal.

And it was happening fast, our populace dwindling even more than it had dwindled from all the other horrors, the wars and the pox and the cannibalism.

The only way we're going to avoid the grafted end times is by crossing the chasm, actually setting foot in that green world where every berry doesn't contain traces of poison, where flowers don't offgas chemicals slumbering in the soil beneath.

Some in our small town listen to me.

Some do not.

Some are willing to leave, to drop down the ladder and try to ford the sea of corrupt flesh.

Some prefer to wait for what is to come, to join the Watchers in their cryptic calendars, that final sight anchoring consciousness, heaven glimpsed for all eternity though feet never travel the winding paths of splendor.

One month. That is what I give my followers. My friends and relatives and occasional rivals. One month to prepare, to gather a life into a pack, to learn how to defend oneself, to obtain the means to defend oneself. The pilgrimage has been made before. Or so it's said. But who can ever believe a story?

Slow death or possible salvation.

Those are the only two options left.

So we leave in one month.

I pray we are ready.

2. Breeze

Mom says we're leaving. Mom says Dad is already in the pit. Mom says there was no way we could have saved him. Mom doesn't say how it happened, or why, or which of the cannibal gods cursed us. All she says is we're leaving with Merek and the others, that there isn't much time.

You can hear them, down there at night. The cries. The animal barks. The yowling and cackling and throaty warble. It's why I first walked to the edge. Mom would kill me if she knew, but I thought I heard Dad's voice, thought I caught his pleading tongue on the wind, lifted from the beasts below. I took the binoculars from one of the dead Watchers. He didn't need them anymore. The moon was full, so I had the silver light to go by. I sat, legs dangling over the edge, peering into the thousand thousand flailing limbs so far below, looking for my father's kind face, for his gaunt body, for whatever was left of him before his skin became the skin of another.

We drank the same water. Ate the same meat. Played soccer each night. Worked the garden each morning.

We only slept one room apart.

I didn't know why it would come for him. Why it wouldn't come for me.

Dad would have been able to help mom cross. He was strong, good with a blade, quick with a thought. I'm small. I know how to urge plants to grow from our sick soil, but little else. That's all I thought I'd ever need to know. How to get the beans to sprout, the potatoes to thicken, the onions to resist the rot. So few in our town have a green thumb, cursed gardens foresting most backyard plots. I knew my life's trajectory, at least before our neighbors started to disappear. Before they started to reappear. Now, all of my garden beds will be abandoned. One final harvest, seeds saved for future sewing, and down the ladder.

Through the binoculars, I saw the bulk of a bear with a dog's head rising from its back, jaws snapping and snapping. I saw a flock of vultures tumbled together, wings only good to jostle them against the hard-packed soil. I saw things that should still live in the ocean, though the ocean is hundreds of miles away and full of toxins. Tentacles. Beaks. Eyes once intelligent, now muted.

There were the men and women, bare skin turning green, all breeds of life fused to their bodies in a pulpy organic mass. Some traveled on all fours. Others were left with a single functioning arm to pull themselves along the dust. At once, they seem separate, but at others, I have trouble telling one from the next. It's as if some thin sinew runs between all, many organisms trapped in one organism, but I don't know. It was dark out, impossible to see clearly.

It must have been hours before I saw my father. I didn't know what the thing that now rode his back had once been. Turtle or amphibian or newborn cow? He struggled to lift the weight, to stumble forward, eyes dead, raised to the moon, face washed in silver.

I couldn't mistake the pain.

When we go down there, I'll save him the only way we know how. Merek has been handing out the pikes, the daggers tied to rake handles, improvised spears of weather-hardened wood. Long-distance weapons he calls them. *Keeps them at bay.* But I don't want to keep my father at bay. I want to let him see heaven, not remain trapped below.

If he had only seen fit to train me with a blade instead of just playing games, kicking the rope ball endlessly around our plot...

A month is rarely enough time to learn.

3. Hearth

Scientists predicted the fault line would calve, sending a third of the continent into the ocean, drowning millions. When the quake hit, the fault split, but nothing fell away. Only the chasm opened, separating one world from the next by a few thousand feet, one continent made into two. It is said that early on, some migrated from one side to the next, to be with whatever family members survived, to seek out the rich lands in the north, but that was before the amalgams were herded, jabbed and prodded over the cliff's edge. No one wanted their toxic bodies decaying in their backyard. No one wanted to burn their flesh for fear of inhaling their disease. Out of sight, out of mind.

But now they're on everyone's mind.

Merek and Gail and Beth have handed out the improvised pikes, all manner of pointy objects fastened to poles: broken bottles, lawn mower blades, honed car bumpers. They teach thrusts. They teach parries. They teach sweeping arcs.

The weapons are ill fitting in most hands. I can't get the hang of it, my movements too slow, which is why I've volunteered to be a mule. I have the bulk, the broad shoulders to carry the load of our caravan. People are sorting through their lives, determining which relics will make the trip from one home to the next, or one home to their grave, depending on how we fare. Necessities come first. Water jugs and cooking pans. Flint. Bedrolls. Rain slickers. Bows and arrows, any hunting implements we can gather. But I've seen the odd vain addition. The cracked mirrors. The family journals passed down from the times when printing presses still ran. Religious reliquaries of uncorrupted flesh. Dead electronics.

After Merek's lesson, Breeze comes to me with a framed photo of her father's great great great grandfather, image water stained and faded. The man looks just like her dad. At least, like he did before he changed, before his skin became shared.

"This is the only thing I care about," she says. "Can you find room?"

I look to my pack, the heap of items stacked one on top of the other, wrapped in an old blue tarp and canvas fabrics, thin ropes encircling the mess. She hands me the photograph. I nod.

"I'll make it fit," I reply. "Can't leave dad behind."

"That's not the plan," she replies, her words grim for a teenager. Something else lingers beneath the surface.

"But you can hold on to it for now. We have time before we go. Would you prefer that?" I ask.

Breeze looks down to the fading image, her father's ghost staring back at her. She shakes her head.

"I don't think I can keep looking at him," she replies. "I know what I'm doing. This will be the memory I keep for the other side."

And she hands me her great great great grandfather before scurrying off to the crumbling house she and her mother inhabit, to that thick green garden that marks their land as different from their neighbors'. I hope she brings seeds with her when we go. A photograph is nice, but if you're starving, there's little nutritional value in waxy, time-worn paper.

I'll remind her before we leave.

I will always have room in my pockets for seeds.

4. Watcher

The trees are as tall as a building stacked on top of a building stacked on top of a building stacked on top of another. They are immense. Belonging to the past. Trunks swollen, roots thick. I no longer have measurements for such. The canopies open, shading what grows in the understory, a rooftop of wide undulating leaves, green on top of green on top of green. If my binoculars were stronger, I might sight the swollen berries growing on groundward shrubs, their pink and blue and yellow skin. But I only have stories, the words Hearth remembers for us all. So my eyes remain in the canopy, with the birds and the mammals with their prehensile tails, their grasping claws and footpads. I imagine myself sitting beside them in the high boughs. Occasionally sparrows land on my shoulder. Occasionally they drop berries in my lap. Vines drape down into heavy thickets. Pitcher plants swarm with flies, nectar rich. Woven bird nests hang from crowns. The ground is covered in rotting mulch, nutrients deep, keeping growth swelling, keeping life in their bark-wrapped limbs. Unlike our soil. Our soil only breeds monsters. Breeds death. I've heard Merek talk about leaving. I've heard their timeframe. I won't be joining them. I won't be leaving my seat. I know the last image I want to see, the last land I want to inherit. And that is not down there, with them, torn limbless by those we threw away.

Heaven awaits those who watch.

There is no other heaven to be had.

5. Breeze

Does Hearth think I'm stupid? Really? Does he think I'm dumb? Does he not know a farmer's most valued possession? I've gathered the seeds. Thousands of seeds. Filled burlap pouches. Every applicable container. The beans. The sprouting potatoes. The kale and the turnip and the peppers. He's not the only one with pockets. He didn't need to say what he did, regardless of how well intentioned he may be. I just didn't want my father's father's father's father's father's photo to get destroyed. Seeds are resilient. Their shells are hard, skin made to endure. They won't shatter as I drive my spear into the throat of whatever comes for us. They won't tear as I hunt the man I need to hunt. (I don't like to think of him as my father anymore, I don't like to think of his name, not with that thing melded to his back.) Beans that spill can be gathered again. The next crop can replenish anything lost to the soil. Pods from pods. Flowers from flowers. Once the photo is gone, then he is gone, and that is the wrong ending. I don't want my final image of my father to be the one I know I will encounter below.

My palms are callus crusted. Each finger joint swollen, blisters cracked, blood dried about my knuckles. Merek has us carve away at the dead trees of the Petrified Forest. Bark is stripped, wood hardened from drought, skin cauterized by the constant beat of the cloudless sun, more stone than pliant pulp. I stab and stab and stab until I feel like I'm going to throw up, visualizing the amalgams, the fleshy chests and necks, those spots where a spear can be driven deep. I never put my father's face where it needs to be, though I know I should. Merek never mentions him. He has no idea. I won't tell him. As I swing my blade into the trunk, wood chips spray like arterial blood. They catch in my hair, coat my skin in a second oaken skin.

"Muscle memory," Merek says, placing a palm on my shoulder. "The more you slash, the more it will feel like you were meant to slash. Your body remembers."

The man is large, but soft in the middle. I don't know why he believes he is the one destined to lead us across the gorge, but no one else threw their name in the ring, so it is Merek, with his long arms and receding hairline, those scars on his neck from when we threw the last amalgam over the cliff. He'd gotten too close, had seen something in its eyes he said he couldn't quite place, something familiar. Something he once loved. A childhood dog? The nurturing look of an aunt? And the amalgam lashed out and took a little bit of him as it tumbled out of sight. I remember the blood and the screaming, but it was just blood and screaming. Nothing worse followed the creature down. Now Merek gets to act as if he is god-branded, as if the knotted skin is a sign of divine touch.

And maybe it is. Who am I to say otherwise?

"Where'd you learn the movements?" I ask, knowing that Merek has been one of our town's guards since before I was born.

He pauses, chews his lip. "My father," he eventually says.

I hate when they do that. Like every mention of the word father is going to send me into a spiral. I've come to terms with where he is. With what he is. I am like the seeds. Stone-skinned. Resilient. That's what Mother says. I don't know how Merek can't see this, but then again, is it a surprise? He saw something once where it never should have been and it almost cost him his life. A blind leader isn't the best. I'm not sure others see him this way, but I see him this way, even though he corrects my swipe, teaches me how to place weight behind a thrust. Just because you see some, doesn't mean you see all.

"And you're almost there. My top student," Merek says, casting a sidelong glance at Lilith, and Benji, and Carp, and Jude, all of whom have sweat through their shirts, their own trees nowhere near as carved as my own. "They're going to rely on you while we're down there, you know that, right?"

"We will rely on each other," I reply, because this is what I know he wants to hear. "We will all get through, I'm sure of it."

"That's the attitude to have," Merek says, patting my shoulder once again. "Keep it up."

Then he's off, down the line, helping Benji raise his cut higher, guiding Lillith on proper foot placement and shoulder rotation.

If I know anything, it's that not all of us are going to make it across. But no one says that out loud. To do so would be to speak those endings into existence. They would become real. Not a possibility. A certainty. And no one wants certainty. Not that certainty anyway. No. We prefer the positive, the fantasy, the waiting utopia.

Merek will lead us across.

Some of us, anyway.

6. Amanda

We can see the stars through the hole in our roof. Sagging beams and torn shingles only obscure a handful of constellations. They slowly track across the sky as I listen to Breeze pad out into the night, as if I don't hear her escape, as if I don't know where she's been going, how she spends her evenings. They were close. Inseparable. I've heard him, too. His voice was with me long before it was with her, long before she was a thought in either of our heads. I wouldn't miss his tenor, even though it was mixed all in with those other gasps and horrid howls. But I let her go. Upon morning, I pretend I don't notice. But I lie awake, listening. The gulch isn't far from our front door. I'd be at her side in a moment if she needed me. But she is getting older and she needs time to herself, to say goodbye to him however she must. There's no easy erasure. She carries her spear. Merek said she is a natural, I need not worry. It's some comfort, but she is so small, and some of those amalgams below are so big. You can only stab so much, slash through so much skin. But it's leave or be consumed in a whole different manner of consumption. The amalgams. The cults. So we will leave. I watched, but didn't watch, my husband become one of them. I won't watch my daughter do the same.

I lie back, fingers entwined behind my head, flickering pin-pricks of light swarming above, ringed in decaying construction materials. I trace their lives, all those flickering years away, until I'm jolted upright by a scream. At once it sounds like Breeze. At another, it does not. It's everyone. It's no one. Regardless, I run, swipe my own spear from beside our doorway, because Merek has been teaching all of us, not just the youths.

Through the doorway, I sprint in the direction where land gives way, to where I know my daughter spends her nights with what's left of her father.

7. Merek

The creature had been a mule. Had been a boar. Had been something with wings which it could no longer use to fly. The beak is still there. So are the tusks. The numerous hooves and horns and dripping mouths.

I've never had to kill something so big.

The Watcher's scream called me from my home, the way withered vocal cords pierced the night stillness. The Watcher hadn't seen the amalgam's shambling approach, only so many breaths left in their lungs, only so many calories left to move-ment. And would they have looked away if they had known? Would they risk that final glance landing on the unsightly instead of their promised kingdom? I don't know. But I do know the beast plowed into their seated form, open wounds and necrotic flesh adhering to their wasted body, human form plucked and stitched and sewn and joined in an instant as muscles fused, as skin grafted, as another four scrambling limbs coalesced with the dozen other protrusions clambering off the central node of torso.

Breeze stands a ways off, mother by her side. Both have spears, but neither move to do what needs doing.

The amalgam thrashes, off balance, the additional un-life bulky and awkward. The Watcher's eyes remain on the horizon, on distant trees, not giving in to the communal pull, life blending with life. Their screams don't abate.

The rest of town slowly funnels out, drawing near the cliff-side. We haven't had a show in months. It's a teachable moment. Some have their weapons. Some come empty handed. I'm disappointed by the latter. Hearth stands there, shouldering his pack, as if we are to embark tonight, as if the screams are a rallying call to begin our pilgrimage. But they aren't. They are warning sirens, a reminder of why we need to leave.

"You have to remember, they aren't quick," I call to the crowd, stepping closer, spear outstretched. "It won't take much to immobilize."

But there are so many legs, so many more than I'm used to.

The doubt is always there, despite the surety of my words.

"Will someone help?" I ask. "This is the moment to prepare for what's to come."

Breeze steps from her mother's side, as I knew she'd step from her mother's side.

"It's hearts and throats. Hearts and throats," I repeat.

She nods and slices through the nearest chest, to no avail. The Watcher continues to scream, eyes unblinking, knowing what is to come, but no longer knowing. There is little we can do to ease their pain. Little beyond swiftness. Talons reach, swipe the air near our faces, but the creature possesses no depth perception. Too many eyes. They stumble, momentum carrying forward, closer to the cliff's edge.

Breeze lifts her spear and drives it through the throat of the once-boar. Instantly, four of the creature's legs go still, head drooping.

The Watcher continues to howl.

I push her aside and jam my pike through the throat that had once belonged to the man that was no longer a man, the man who had been someone's son, someone's brother or father or friend. Every death ripples.

The scream is swallowed.

Then Breeze levels another cut.

Another set of legs stop moving.

With a last gash, I sever the once-mule's head, and the thing falls still. I give it a nudge with the blunt end of my spear, say a prayer on its passing. None of these creatures wanted this. None of them deserve such a ragged fate, the endless pain and suffering. There is no groan, no twitch of muscle.

"And that's it," I say, pointing at Breeze, pointing at the now truly dead thing. "Easy enough."

And the crowd cheers. They've seen my words morph into reality. They know it can be done. That it can be done easily. We aren't descending the ladder to our graves. We aren't going to become like them. Faith is restored. Faith flourishes. They clap and howl and scream, voices becoming indistinguishable from the noise rising from below. We are going to make it. That's what I've told them, again and again. The more I speak those words, the more I believe them myself, the more I can push down my own dark projections. The unknown distance. The wall of mouths and tusks and wounds. All that fetid blood, the hungry flesh.

I'll keep saying those words, certainty summoned from lack.

Morale has never been higher, which is important. We leave soon, sooner than any of us would like.

8. Breeze

One amalgam is simple. A thousand thousand amalgams is not.

9. Hearth

They bring me their packs, asking advice, how to best fit the most in their limited spaces. Canteens and shovels and dried meat and spare footwear. I've gone through their belongings, item by item, analyzing which fits best, each a puzzle piece with no easy attachment. Only one has brought actual puzzle pieces, the image of a calm lake with a hundred kittens lazing about the shore. She said it was her grandmother's, that she's kept it wrapped in a waterproof ziplock through generations, the plastic slowly eroding over the years.

I can't fault the desire to bring entertainment. To bring comfort.

If life is limited to necessities, where will we find joy?

Others have acoustic guitars, fiddles, the steel xylophone keys inked with the name of a high school that hasn't been a high school in years. There are paperback mysteries, Stephen King horrors, romances set in countries that are no longer countries. So much is not what it once was.

I show them how to tether each, how to keep the waterproofing tarps tight to prevent the rain, if there ever was rain, from soaking everything they love.

I speak encouragement. Helping smooth second guesses, those that waiver, those that wonder aloud if they should stay behind.

To stay behind is to die.

To move on is to live.

I've said this a thousand times in the past weeks: my own personal mantra. There's nothing false in the statement. Statistically, at the rate amalgams claim our neighbors, our village won't last more than a few more years. We will all be grafted. We will all be part of the thing that writhes below.

That, or the cannibal cults will roam through, asking for offerings.

To offer is always better than to withhold.

To lose a little is preferable to losing all.

I lead the others around our town, packs hoisted on shoulders, getting them accustomed to the weight. We put miles beneath boot heels, looping and looping, the same sights on repeat. The crumbling houses. The fifty-gallon water barrels outside each. The dry fountains and swimming pools. The withered gardens. The storefronts that are no longer storefronts, *Closing Sale* signs leaning in shattered windows. There are the carcasses of cars and school buses, bikes with flattened tires, heaps of rusting metal I can no longer remember the purpose of, plastic sun-bleached, wood given way to dry rot.

We pass the flock of desert turkeys that haunt the outskirts of town, the malnourished deer that jolt away at our footsteps.

We don't pass much else that still draws breath.

"How far will it be?" a young boy asks, adjusting the pack that is almost equal to his height.

"Not far. Not farther than we have traveled today," I reply.

"I'm glad. I don't know how much farther I can run," the boy says as we continue on.

He stumbles and goes down on one knee.

I place a hand beneath his armpit, steadying his rise. I won't tell him if this happens below, he'll be on his own. No one will have the chance to help. Everyone will be helping themselves, a flock unable to save every fledgling, but he doesn't have to know this. The only preparation is to train. If I can get it just right, he won't fall again. His legs will be strong. His back will be strong. He won't be one of those swept away in that sea of limbs and teeth.

"Just a little farther," I say. "Just a little farther."

10. Watcher

They will leave soon. I hear it in their step, in the way their voices near and retreat. I know they stare down into the pit, envisioning their future below, planning routes, envisioning traps. I know they look upon all that has been warped, the clambering mouths, the talons reaching towards the sky. But that is not where they should be looking. No. They should hold their gaze to the horizon, to that undulating sea of green. To die with the vines in your sight is to live forever in the land's verdant arms. Let the trees hold you. Let the birds lift you in flight. Let the shade cast off the sun's constant scorn. Let the rain soak your skin, fill your mouth with clean joy. This is all the last sight will grant. This is all we pray for. Merek has offered each of us a place in his ranks. I've heard him move down the length of the cliff, stopping at each chair, reciting the same plea. Yes, we know what happened to our brother down the way. We know what might happen to each of us. But the days grow on, and I grow tired.

My legs will not carry me down the ladder. My hands will not hold the pike. Muscle no longer exists where it once flourished. Merek should know this. All I have left is the sight, the next life waiting for me in better soil. We appreciate the sentiment, the care, but the time for change is long past. Merek's offer comes too late. If he knew what was good for him, he'd pull up a chair, raise the binoculars to his eyes, and welcome the sight. Nothing else is going to welcome him.

11. Breeze

I step into the street, rough sand beneath my boots, easing the door closed behind. Night has fallen. There is a man there, back to me, shirtless, already tracing the path I will follow. His skin moves, undulates. He is no longer a man. I shouldn't use that word. A hundred mice wriggle on his back and shoulders, exposed calves and neck, many bodies becoming one body. I am sure if he were to fall, human legs no longer able to bear the weight, the mice feet would carry him to the cliffs, to where the others call to their kin, a body carried as if on a shallow tide. I grip my spear tighter. Do I cut or do I simply follow?

The man is crying. It's subtle, but unmistakable. The tears. Comprehension still tethered despite everything. Thought still runs through the singular mind. They drag forward, step after step, tears leaving a breadcrumb map to their next life. They weep for our mistakes, for what we could have had but foolishly discarded. They weep for themselves. No one wants to admit this is their life, that this is their fate.

I stay back, trace their path from the shadows, moving house to house, sliding over decaying fencing, feet light on brick walkways. I don't want to startle them. I don't want them to turn and decide they hunger for another body to add to their own. I can afford the risk. It wouldn't take much to cut them down, if the potential threat became an actual threat. One quick throatward jab. But there is something to be learned. I've only seen those that were mostly beast, rarely those that were mostly man, even if that man was buried beneath a sea of rats. They move differently. Quicker. Less mass bearing down on their shared limbs. More direction. More certain

The man's head tilts forward, eyes on the green horizon cast gray by the moonlight. They reach the end of the road, pavement falling to cracked stone, falling to swept sand. There are no more houses for me to hide behind. Just that open expanse, the few seated forms stretching out in either direction, the occasional withered tree, and then the fall. The mouse man isn't headed for a Watcher, isn't set on carrying a second life down with their own. They shamble between two of the seated forms, each a hundred feet apart from the next in their rusting beach chairs.

At the cliff's edge, the mouse man stops, head rising towards the moon, one ear, which is many ears, cocked towards the braying rising below. They are bathed in silver light, illumination catching on all of those tiny white-furred bodies, their paws skittering and clawing at the open air, unable to find purchase. I wonder if there's something he can hear in the tumult that I can't. Language shared by those who no longer remember language. Our language anyway.

The mouse man nods, as if in agreement to the unheard conversation, then takes another step forward, toes cresting the rocky lip.

Then they turn, shifting their gaze towards town, towards the road, where I am left standing. Our eyes meet. There is a moment I think he will charge, an anger spreading across his face, a sadness, hands flexing at sides, those hundred mouse heads trained on me, a hunger in the twitch of their noses, in the chittering of their teeth. I level my spear, placing the honed point between us in a clear statement. I recognize the man in the moonlight. He's Benji's father. Or was Benji's father. I hurt for them, for the realization they will have when they wake tomorrow and he is no longer there, sleeping in the neighboring room, no longer a source of nurturing joy, a memory relegated to the past. How many nights will pass before Benji joins me on the cliffs, listening for their father, trying to decipher that last farewell? Not long, I tell myself.

I adjust my spear, feet planted like Merek said.

The mouse man shakes his head and steps backward off the cliff. The voices of a hundred mice wheeze into the night air, high and keening, as they drop from sight.

I run to the lip, peering down, trying to find the mouse-man/Benji's father in the tumult. There is no bloodstain on the rock, no smear of viscera on the ground. No, the mouse-man is carried aloft by the amalgams beneath, all those beast backs cushioning the fall. All those arms rising to intercept. They are pushed forward, swept along, those around them welcoming the new arrival with their continued thrashing song. Then Benji's dad is swept under, disappearing from sight, no longer an individual, now part of the whole.

Down the length of the cliff, I look to see if any Watchers have glanced away from the distant forest, to track the mouse-man's rebirth, but none have moved. Life goes on around them, though they are no longer part of it. Truth be told, the nearest is dead, head lolling to the side, binoculars dangling from slouched neck. I ease them over their head, lank hair all but falling away from their scalp. I clean the eyepieces under the cuff of my sleeve. I'm not a barbarian. Hygiene is never something to forsake. My theft will leave one less temptation, one less excuse for those who wish to give themselves over to the sight. In a way, I'm saving a life. In a way, I'm providing one more hand to hold a spear. So in that sense, it is selfish, but the Watchers are wrong. They just die. No heaven awaits them. It is either death up here, or death down there, or a better life on the other side, for a time anyway. I don't know how they can't see that, considering they claim to see so much.

12. Hearth

I'm not bringing my father's books, the ones he saved from his father, who saved them from his. The history of our world doesn't need to be carried into the next. The cannibal religions and devouring lands, all those microcosm wars fought by the few who had arms to raise and the disgusting desire to raise them. We won't need the explanations of how we went astray. All we need is one scrap of paper stating *take care of what you have. Never corrupt it. If it doesn't come from the earth, from the trees or from the sky, just let it be.* We know there is some toxic threshold passed in the amalgams, opening their skin, allowing wounds to sucker on to other wounds, two become one become many. It's in the water we drink. In the meals we eat. But in the forest, meals will no longer be the same, the water will weep from different wells. I don't fault others for the books they bring, for the joy the written word represents, but none of our histories bring joy, just sad reminders of how things didn't have to be as they are, that we wouldn't have to make the pilgrimage if we'd just been more kind to the world we'd been given. But we will be kinder to the next.

If we make it to the next.

If the world decides to be kind to us.

13. Merek

Only so many days are left. Benji broke their spear, anger over-coming judgment. There are few unclaimed weapons, so I craft one from what we have. I can't let them climb the ladder with-out protection, not after what happened to their father, mirror image falling back upon him. So I uproot a thin sapling, dead for years, whose skin has been baked into a semblance of steel. There is no spare metal, no glass we're willing to break. Sharp-ening is my only option. A point is all one needs.

"It won't break?" Breeze asks, standing in my front yard, practicing lunges as I carve away at the wood, my lap filling with dried pulp.

"Think of how many strikes it takes you to carve through one of these," I say, raising the partially formed spear like it's still a member of the nearby forest, like there's still hope it might leaf out come spring. "It will serve Benji well enough, especially considering the other option."

"Empty hands aren't ideal," Breeze replies, breathing heavily. Another slash. Another thrust. Another parry.

"But you'll keep them at bay. You know that. If Benji sticks close, they'll make it across in your shadow."

"I'd prefer to have them at my side rather than behind me, thank you very much."

"Some need to be leaders. Others followers. One can't play every role. You know which camp you belong to."

She grunts a reply, impaling an imaginary adversary, amalgam limbs falling still beneath her movements.

"You don't have to give me an answer now, but I'd like you to be one of the first to climb down with me, to secure the ladder's base. I can think of few better suited to..."

"Yes. I don't need to think about it," she says.

"Aren't you worried?"

"Yeah, of course I am. But I'm probably less worried than the rest. I see quite a few dropped spears and soiled shorts in our future."

I can't resist the laugh.

"But not from you. Never from you."

"You know that," she says with a smile. "I've got a bladder of steel."

At first, I didn't think Breeze liked me. I couldn't put my finger on why. If there was something I said, or did. But in the past weeks, she's been showing up outside my door, after training, asking for more training, advanced techniques as if I know anything beyond the basic movements my father taught me. I just emphasize the fundamentals. Energy coming, energy going. Balance and leverage.

I'd always wondered what it would have been like to have a child of my own. If they were anything like Breeze, I'd be proud, but that is a reality unstuck from my own, sad as it might be. I don't kid myself into thinking I'm a stand-in for her father, the man descended from that man in the photo she gave to Hearth for safe keeping. No. I'm just the only guy who has a vague understanding of what we need below, what we need to do to climb that second ladder. And she values this. Breeze is smart. She wouldn't waste her time on me otherwise.

"Are you sure?" I ask, giving her a final out.

"Absolutely," she replies, a final jab to punctuate her sentence.

14. Amanda

The night before we leave, I sit beside Breeze, our legs dangling over the cliff's edge, listening for my husband below. She extends a second pair of binoculars I didn't know she had. The moon has dwindled, so there is little light to go by. Dark undulating shadows roil below, arms and heads rise out of the turmoil, man and beast and bird, visible one moment, swallowed the next. I alternate between sight and sound, eye tilted down, ear tilted down. I can't find him down there. No sign whatsoever.

"Maybe he's truly dead," I say, lowering the binoculars to my lap, unsure if this is a hopeful comment or a mordant one.

"I don't think so. I heard him last night," Breeze replies, moving her pair back and forth in a slow canvasing scrawl, pausing for a moment, then continuing on.

"A single day can make all the difference," I say.

She knows what I mean.

One day my husband was himself, making jokes about the oddly shaped gourds Breeze had been growing in the garden, this one phallic, that one like a giant bulbous bottom. Then the next dragging himself to the pit, that creature melded to his back, rider to mount, lips no longer lush with jokes, or kind words, or our own practiced love language. His voice had been swallowed along with his future. I didn't see it happen. I didn't hear him leave as I do with Breeze each night. He must have met that thing out there on midnight wander, ever restless like his daughter, a chance encounter to end all chance encounters. I only saw the shadow of the thing that tumbled down over the cliff, the warped man who had been the only person I'd slept next to for the last twenty years. My only true home at the end of the world.

She doesn't need me to spell this out.

She doesn't need me to say anything, yet I feel like I can't keep my tongue to myself anymore, I can't hold all the emotions inside.

"I miss him, Bee. I miss him so much," I say.

"I know, Mom. It's impossible not to," she replies.

"Do you think it's ever going to feel any better?"

A mother asking for mothering. Not my best turn.

There is a sharp intake of breath, an almost sad exasperation from my daughter. I never know who lost more, she or I?

"Better is hard to say. I'm going to fix this as much as I can. It will never be what it was, but we won't have to be out here listening to him crying," Breeze says, binoculars halting in their wander.

"What do you mean by..."

"He's right there," she says, cutting me off, finger extended down into the gorge.

I follow her direction, bringing the lenses up to my eyes. And there he is, surfacing for a moment, anguish painted on his face, mouth open in a howling O, just like the reptilian thing whose skin he shares, their own face appearing above his, just over the shoulder. Their faces mirror one another. Neither knows comfort. Neither knows joy.

The wind changes direction, bringing with it the fetid breath from below. Dung and blood and rot and the sickly ripe scent of turned grapes. I gag, drop the binoculars back into my lap. That isn't the smell I want to associate with my husband, the last sensory impression he makes. I prefer to think of his breath, of his sweat, of his mouth after we drank cactus wine by the old dried river at the edge of town.

I won't press Breeze on what she meant. I know she plans with Merek. I know that the others look to her for advice, for strength. She's allowed to be cryptic, given what we are walking into tomorrow.

She's a smart girl.

She wouldn't do anything stupid.

15. Watcher

The only time I have dropped my gaze was to observe them leave. In truth, my forest is there, in the background, the backdrop for their exodus, so, it can be said that my eyes were still held by the almighty, by the world to come. Temptation didn't lead me astray. I wanted to see. Wanted to know. Some of them had been my friends. Some my family. Merek had whispered in my ear the day before, a final plea, a final promise. He's kind to all, symbolic as the gesture was. We all know none of my fellow Watchers are making the pilgrimage, not the physical pilgrimage, to be precise. But our pilgrimage drags on, nonetheless. We will see them when they arrive. Some of us will be there to meet them when hands find that final ladder rung. Some of us are already there.

16. Breeze

The rope is brittle for stretches, slick for others. An occasional length feels like it's going to give way to rot, soft under my clenched fists. Others are coated in dried blood, in misplaced viscera. I try not to think of how it got there as I climb down, as my spear taps against my back, the fabric tethering the weapon in place allowing for little movement. My pockets bulge with seed packets, kale and potato and onion and pepper crammed into burlap and canvas and plastic. They shake like tiny maracas, keeping time with my descent.

Merek is beneath me. Beneath him are the amalgams, milling about, seemingly unaware of our arrival. I've heard Hearth speak about how, while their bodies inhabit our shared world, their minds no longer view the same physical plane. He says when they act out in violence, it's not an intentional aggression, just a reflex, possibly the answer to something unspooling in their other realm. Either way, it doesn't matter. Their claws are claws. Their teeth are teeth. Intention, at that point, doesn't matter. The mouseman clearly stared at me on the night he took his dive. Maybe they move between realms? Maybe Hearth's theories are false. Not all of his ideas are anchored in reality, but at least he tries to make sense of things. It's more than most can say.

As we descend, the stench rises around us. The death. The decay. The rotting fruit and wilted flowers. I pull my shirt over my nose. I don't know how much the fabric shield will help when we wade in, but it's all I have. A green scrim of light drifts down, sun casting rays through the leaf canopy on the other side of the gorge, a reminder of why we are here, why we risk so much. The other side isn't far away. I can see the second rope ladder rising up, a beacon of twined fibers, vague in the distance.

Merek's boots touch sand. In a fluid motion, his spear is unslung, point leveled at the nearest monstrosity, an amalgam of ox and bear and rooster and possum. It is huge, but doesn't seem to notice our landing, only pushes on, pressing against the next nearest beast, who pushes into the next nearest beast, all of which are howling, all of which are a tumult of mismatched limbs grasping for some world they can't hold onto. The mass moves as one, as if they are all entwined, one beast equal to all beasts.

Then I am down, mimicking Merek's arrival. Spear out, pack adjusted, shirt still over my nose. The claw of a nearby amalgam soars over my head, almost clipping the man above me on the ladder. I dip to the side and plunge my spear into one of the creature's necks, the offending limbs falling still, a splash of blood curdling in the dirt at my feet. There is a grunt, a sad release of breath.

"We need to hurry," Merek says, looking up the ladder.

"I don't think we have much of a choice," I reply.

Another man is down, then another, then a woman, all un-slinging spears from their backs, all awash in terror.

We walk in an expanding half circle, pushing back the boundaries of our landing camp, nudging the amalgams out of the way, killing those that refuse to move. The air is sharp with copper. Constant curses are muttered. A man screams and falls silent, body pulled away from the rest of us. A name is wailed, a flurry of unhinged swipes spread through our number, an initial attempt to reclaim our lost, but the creatures don't part. They absorb the blows, dying and not dying, refusing to give the man back. Someone sobs to my left. I yearn to comfort, to place a reassuring hand on a shoulder, but I need my hands for the spear. Hopefully that shoulder will still be there for comforting when we reach the other side, hopefully still attached.

Benji steps into the hole the man abandoned. They shake, spear tip jostling side to side, eyes flicking every which way.

"Calm is the only way you're making it," I tell them as I thrust my spear into a mass of flesh I can't make sense of, just the writhing limbs, a flailing tail, a neck that climbs up and up. "Breathe in. Breathe out. Just do as Merek taught and you'll be alright."

They nod and spear a monstrosity to my right, Merek's recently sharpened tip coming away crimson.

Part of me watches those descending.

Part of me watches the beasts die beneath our spears, the ones that lash out, slicing a man in half, ripping a woman's calf from the rest of her leg. With each dead, there is a faltering, a hesitancy to step forward. Those around look back to the ladder, to the way we've come, but fear doesn't overcome muscle memory, drills and repetition running through limbs without thought Retreat is tempting, dread howling in all our ears, but the body moves on.

———

I search for my father between lunges and parries.

His face hasn't peered out from the quivering wall of receding flesh. I've seen other human faces, their skin mottled, lips lost, bare-teeth-rictus always spread wide. But never across his warped features. I don't know how I'm going to find him. I don't know if he's even a sentient entity in the way I categorize sentient entities. The sea of bodies before us looks more and more like a single organism, lines of sinew and bone connecting one to all, a roving mass of membrane. They can shift and stroll, but something always seems connected. And it would make sense. If one creature could bond to the next and the next and the next, why would the process stop? We're just carving our way through the final sin of the human race, the boney, gelatinous, muscle-rich wasteland of the pit, every species coming to the same place to die, but not die.

———◦———

I kill four amalgams, and none of them. Their muted bodies are dragged back from our perimeter, out of sight, reabsorbed by the shivering organism.

My father is part of the throng.

I hear his voice to the left, his screaming, his cry. It reminds me of a twisted ankle when we were kicking the ball around the garden, but worse, like vocal cords had grown additional vocal cords to express the lament. I can't stand this.

I turn, about to wade into the writhing tide, but Merek's hand finds my shoulder, eyes following my gaze into the storm of bodies and bodies.

"I asked you to join me first to perform a job. Don't get distracted. Those behind are dependent on your next decision," he says, eyes flicking to the last person who has slipped off the ladder, our final pilgrim in this final pilgrimage. "The lost are already lost. There's nothing you can do about that."

"I know," I reply, turning from my father's vocalization. "I'm sorry."

I apologize, but I don't mean the words.

I have one job now, but the second job will still be there when I am finished. I don't need to tell him this. I just need to hold up my end of the bargain. For now.

"No need to apologize. Just keep pushing. The other ladder isn't that far."

And he's right, I can see the faint outline of it in the distance, climbing the rockface, swaying gently in the fetid wind.

Far is a relative measurement considering what roves before us.

17. Hearth

Merek and Breeze and the other women and men carve a corridor for those behind. The other mules and I heave our weight in their wake, packs stacked high, possessions crammed in the most orderly way I could manage, one atop the next atop the next. We are careful to avoid the constant inward press of the amalgams, the way their forms want to coalesce and fill the vacated space. It's like a dam holding back a river on two sides, a river made of sickly meat. I think of my father's texts, those tomes I left behind. Maybe they would have been helpful after all? Maybe I'd be able to make true sense of the surreality that is my reality?

On either side are a wall of dead, and not so dead, eyes. They stare as we pass, peering out from faces once belonging to horse and swine and pigeon and frog, men and women emerging from beasts, friends and lovers lost to the pit. They track steps, mouths falling open. Not in hunger. More of a question. More a desire that can't flit from a tongue. Part of me doesn't believe they comprehend what they witness, that their minds are elsewhere, but it is hard to hold that claim when eyes lock, when a flicker of recognition passes over that cornea.

I will remember this. Remember it all. Tell the story of what we've witnessed.

To my right, a man named Frank is dragged into the writhing mass by his ankle. There are screams, the sound of something wet and slurping, like something being devoured, like something being reborn. Benji jabs their spear into the nearest body, and the wall shifts back, receding a foot, two, giving us space to continue, not allowing us to retrieve our dead.

We knew there were going to be dead.

That was never a question.

The only question was, what would be their names?

Lorna?

Fil?

Amanda?

Breeze?

Hearth?

It was a list none wanted to dwell on. It was a list we prayed only our neighbors' names appeared on, the neighbors we were least close with. And that felt bad enough. We were all muttering our own incantations beneath our breath. Some speaking to the cannibal gods of old, others to the angels that came before them, the Old one whom many said was worshiped across continents, God with a capital G. I've read all the records I can, ingested each crumb of history. I know They rarely answered the call before, the Cannibals, the Gods. So why would they now?

For those reasons, I have no prayers.

I just have my knowledge, and my remembrances of books, and my faith in Merek and those out front, and everything that waits for me on the other side.

New knowledge isn't that far from our reach. New stories. New narratives.

I step and I step and I step.

Avoid the claw. Avoid the tooth.

There is little else to think of below.

Only progress.

18. Amanda

Is it wrong that the daughter carries the spear for the mother? That the mother isn't out front, protecting the daughter, rather than in the back of the caravan, pack laden, ferrying our old life into our new, no weapon in hand, weapon given to another with more strength to place behind the thrust. I should feel more of an instinct. More of a desire to preserve my child. But my child is stronger than I am. My child is a natural with a spear in hand.

As she silences the groping arms of what had once been a man who lived a few houses down, I think of her as a child, not the mostly grown near-woman before me. I think of hours in the garden. Small fingers plowing through soil, nudging seeds into loam. Long trips to the water font, the close-to-dry well at the end of town. All those sloshing buckets, all those promises of what the soil will yield. Breeze understood something intuitively. Hearth only told her so much, only recounted the basic necessity of water and sun and depth and nutrients. The rest seemed to flourish in her fingertips, as if in a past life she had kept the gardens of the rich, the mythic arboretums supposedly still existing out East, in the North, where the rain is still rain and the amalgams don't wander the undergrowth.

I can see her squatting there with her father, pinching dead leaves and suckers off tomato plants, stripping mildewed growth off squash. He nudges her playfully and she tips on her side, playing into the comedy, rolling on her back, turtle-like, throwing clods of dirt at his chest. It impacts, spraying sediment, drawing a smile. There is a momentary war of flung sod, until he steps on a seedling and Breeze raises a halting hand.

I think I'm done now, she said.

My husband looked down at the crushed growth.

I think I am too, he said, before they plucked the dead seedling, replacing it with a fresh seed, old life replenished with new.

I don't like the new life I see around me. It pulls me from recollections, pleasant memories of the place that had once been the only safe place we'd ever known. But he's not there anymore. He's down here, skin added to the skin of all, this bulging mass of connected beings, every species pulled together, stitched like a mad scientist 's experiment, a necromancer's unfounded desire become whole. It's all inversion. All warped. My husband was never supposed to become what masses around us, the limbs that flee at my daughter's thrusts and stabs, the bulk of chest and muscle that no longer make articulate sense, biology a dead word on my tongue.

Hearth has tried to explain this, tried to use his father's words to illuminate the dark miracle's curse, but he doesn't really know. Only parts are glimpsed, never the whole.

A splash of blood hits my face. I hurry to wipe the viscous fluid away, not knowing who it belonged to, what their veins contain. With each of our number felled, I shudder under my pack, a blow to one a blow to all. Dread and calm mix in my spine, coalesce in my gut. Without the calm, forward steps are impossible. Without the dread, safety isn't either. Existing in both worlds is a strain, mind threatening to break under carnage, but I can hold.

We haven't long now.

⸻

The ladder isn't far.

The braided fibers sway in the wind, pushed gracefully against the rock face, as if the ladder's dancing, as if it waves in welcome.

I imagine Breeze climbing the rungs over my head. I follow. I imagine the top of the cliff, the new home where she won't have to be this person ever again, soaked in blood, hunks of gore woven into her hair. This is not what any mother wants for their child. This is the end of something that may never have been there, only an illusion, a belief clung to like a prayer, like a curtain shielding the world from unknowing eyes. But there is no curtain. Only blood and grasping limbs. Innocence is a thing belonging to the past.

A woman is dragged away.

A hoof nearly catches Hearth's shoulder.

Breeze ducks beneath the snapping jaws of some giant cat-goat.

I walk on, adjusting my pack, envisioning the climb to come.

19. Merek

We have lost less than I imagined. Fifty percent survival would have been a hope. A dream. I don't have time for head counts, but I'm thinking seventy-five percent. Three-fourths survival. I've trained our front well, spears skewering in a plodding phalanx, ground gained, the mass that is all pushed back again and again, the corridor widening, the final stretch ahead. My arms ache. My feet ache. Red razor gashes trace my forearms and neck, mimicking the gash I'd received last year, a reminder of what an unfocused mind can bring. I haven't counted how many have fallen still beneath my spear. The amalgam, singular, as I now know it to be, is a hydra, one head lopped, another two grown back. But it's more like the sea. Ever shifting, ever expanding, tides receding, called by natural forces, no intellect, back and forth, a new environment, a new corrupted landscape. We are the first explorers of this new terrain. Hopefully we won't be the last.

I'm glad to see those that follow. I'm glad to see I didn't lead my friends to their deaths. All of my friends, anyway. I'm glad I wasn't mistaken. They deserved better than they got. They weren't the ones responsible for the amalgams, for what breeds in the soil and weeps from the sky. Few deserve the hand they are dealt. Fate is cruel. Older generations crueler.

I don't know how many more will fall before we reach the ladder. I tell myself it will be few as I skewer more un-life. We are so deep into the mass. I can barely recognize the origins of the flesh, can't name the faces and eyes that stare out at me from the tunnel-like expanse. One undying organism. One unthinking limb forever coiling and uncoiling at the base of this gorge.

I call a word of encouragement.

The word is called back to me.

I love these people.

I love what awaits them on the other side, because they deserve reprieve, as do I.

As does everything that writhes before us.

But not everyone who deserves joy is granted its kiss.

20. Breeze

My father continues to cry. He isn't far off. Neither is the ladder.

Just keep speaking. Keep letting me know you're there.

Where to find you.

I won't be long now.

I won't.

21. Hearth

The ladder shivers beneath my palms as I hold the aged fibers
steady for those that climb, dirt falling into my eyes from clacking boot heels, grit landing in my mouth. Merek has spread a
perimeter. We are encased in spears. The wall of flesh is always
trying to absorb, to claim new limbs, new faces, but the grasping
folds are pushed back, again and again, occasionally dragging a
body away, another name added to the list I try to keep in my
head.

Amanda claws hand over foot, scaling the rope height, the
weight of her pack threatening to pull her down, gravity cruel,
but she will make it. The climb isn't too much. She made it
down the first time. The adrenaline alone should propel her
forward. Seth and Viv and Glenn and Cala and Brye and Lee
follow, one after the next. I will wait until every last carrier has

risen. I whisper words of hope as they climb, attempting to paint the picture of their new life, as they lift their weight for the first rung, praying they will remember those words when they reach the last.

I thought Amanda would have waited as well, waited for her daughter, but I haven't seen Breeze in a time. I scan the gathered fighters. Breeze's long blood-slick hair doesn't flow amongst the others, that fetid gust tangling the strands as it had. I didn't see her fall. Didn't hear her scream. She can't be dead. Not another name for our list. She is the best of us. I must be mistaken.

Then her laugh carries to me on the sour-grape wind, high and trilling.

Though I can't see her, I know she still draws breath, and I know where she has gone.

I've never wanted to know something less in my life.

But still, I will wait.

22. Amanda

She told me not to wait. She told me to trust her when the moment came. She will do this, as much for myself as for her.

I've let her wander many nights alone beneath the moon, out there in the dark, these things crawling all over. I think about following her, grasping her arm, pulling her back from what I know awaits. I know that's what a mother is supposed to do, protect, restrain, comfort, but I also know what Breeze is capable of. What I can't stop.

One day of wandering beneath the sun can't be much worse than all those forgotten midnights.

Not when she has a future she envisions.

Not when she has hope.

23. Merek

Her laugh isn't far. It drops down from above, to my left. It's a lure. A homing siren. Most are up the ladder. My spearbearers have held the line. They look to me, and I wave them off before climbing the mostly-dead wall of flesh. Spear-hole-riddled, a thousand gaping wounds pile one on top of the next. I know she went up. I know she climbed. Not the ladder. A different ladder of sorts. I should have known this would happen, that this was the inevitable conclusion of her story. Find the father. Finish the father. Old ghosts laid to rest. She can't do it alone, not with the endless body beneath her, those flickering limbs shooting up, grasping, attempting to drag her back down into their folds. I stab and climb and stab and climb, more mass stilled, more eyes vacant.

Then I am standing on the thing that is many things that is one thing, boots squelching over flesh and fur, cartilage and bone cracking beneath my feet, slick from sweat and other ex-cretions. Breeze isn't far. I can see clear across the mass, both sides of the cliff looming over us, that green effervescent light floating down from the near, but not so near, forest. The radiance bathes the black and red landscape a sickly verdant hue. I almost have to cover my eyes from the jaded light. I've grown used to the darkness of the almost-body-tunnel, the dark dark pallet.

But I run anyway, ignoring the cry in my heels, the strain in my calves.

I slash at what grasps. I dodge what lunges.

Breeze's father curls back before her, his legs welded to the mass beneath him, appendages woven into one snakelike coil, muscle and tissue of so many beasts wrapped around his form. The thing on his shoulder, that I'd always assumed was some breed of tortoise I'd never encountered in life, is actually another man, or woman, life long given to the disease, all their features appearing melted, skin bubbled, almost scalelike, almost shell-like. The second once-human peers over the first's shoulder, smiling, teeth all but melted away. Where Breeze's father's eyes are off in Hearth's other world, this second man or woman, it is impossible to tell, is clearly present, clearly sharing our reality, enjoying what they see before them. They are so much taller than Breeze, a pillar of flesh, an obelisk climbing towards the sky. She is small in their shadow, in the shadow of the thing that is all things. But she doesn't back down, doesn't cower. Her once-father rises until there is no more height to gain, until he (they?) practically black out the green-tinged sun.

Then they descend, arms and arms reaching for their once-daughter.

Breeze plants her feet like I taught, spear raised, letting the creature do the work. There is no thrust, no muscle-tearing stab. Her father impales himself on the spear's sharp point, Breeze having angled it just right, tip sinking into neck, protruding from skull. She is pushed back in the rush, feet sliding across the mass of lesser bodies, until motion is halted. Her father sags, his collected limbs draping forward, arms swaying, scarecrow-like in the wind, but the other once-man/woman keeps smiling, reaching their hands around their truly dead counterpart. Fingers wrap the shaft of the spear, dragging themselves forward, forcing more of the weapon through their dead second self, dragging itself closer to Breeze, hand over hand.

I am running, no longer halted by the glory that was her final stand, all awe fleeing my thoughts.

I know what it's trying to do.

I know what will happen if I don't intervene.

Breeze struggles to drag the spear free, but the once-man/woman won't let go, only grinds closer, gore-slick palms clasping Breeze's, forearm skin opening, twining muscle reaching from one to the other, suckering on to Breeze's skin, leech-like, worming its way in, pulling her close, two attempting to become one, that sick miracle festering before my eyes.

I lunge, the sharp edge of my spear slicing through the thickening membrane, a torrent of blood soaking my boots, coating Breeze's skin. She screams, and pulls back, spear coming with her. A wet suctioning gasp escapes the wound as she tumbles back, finds her footing once more. Her dead father and the other once-person drift sideways, swinging at me in bellowing rage, still-living mouth flung wide, wider than any human jaw should allow. I dip low, trying to create distance. Something in my leg gives out, a sudden flash of pain radiating out from my knee, a wet pop. And I'm falling, back and back and back and back as the once-person looms, as they collapse forward on that snake stalk of dying tissue.

I'm on my back, ready for the end.

I knew there was a chance of this.

Knew there was a risk.

I'm okay with that.

Not okay with Breeze being on her own again.

Not okay with...

Her spear finds the soft meat of the second neck, Breeze's lunge carrying her over my prone form. There is blood, green fading back to red back to green, the once-person's eyes going wide, moving from the girl, to the spear shaft, to the heavens, before sight grows distant, a life flickering out as the twisted amalgam stills, collapsing on top of its slowly undulating bulk.

A finality.

An actual end.

24. Breeze

Merek is heavy. Only one leg supports weight. I have become his second leg as we struggle across the expanse of amalgam bodies, forearm searing, open blood calling to all the others moaning and chortling and squealing beneath us. Merek uses his free arm to skewer, to press back the encroaching mass piling up around us. With each step, the almost-dead-architecture grows higher, a tunnel forming. A wave threatening to crash. There is an arm thrashing. A hoof intended to maim. A spear finding each in time.

Then we are at the edge of the beasts' bulk, a small cliff before the true cliff. Hearth is there, at the bottom, calling up to us, arms open wide.

"Ease him down. I'll catch him. Trust me."

And I do. The man has done nothing but lug the crushing weight of others' useless belongings for the past month. His back is strong. I unsling Merek, helping him over the lip, kicking back a thin tentacle of an arm, until he can find a foothold. It's three awkward vertical strides and he's falling into Hearth's arms. The two men tumble down into the dirt, sprawled limbs, a torrent of swears. I follow, but land on my own two feet. The two men have already risen, Merek draped over Hearth's shoulders like a human backpack, Merek's injured leg hanging loose to one side. We don't have time to linger, to splint the limb. The wall of once-life drags onward, narrowing our already narrow corridor, the sky growing more distant overheard with lashing arms and roving heads.

We run.

"What about your pack?" I ask. "There's no way I can shoulder it."

"I wouldn't ask you to," Hearth replies. "Nothing inside is worth your life."

The massive wrapped bundle of canvas leans against the cliffside wall, unending spools of rope coursing over the possessions of the living and dead alike. I think about my father's father's father's father's photograph hidden somewhere inside the mound, that smiling face, the face I hadn't found out in the amalgam wasteland. I don't think I could ever look at it again. My eyes would show me one thing, my brain another. Memory can't be cleansed, regardless of the tangible evidence before me. All of him will remain in the gorge, severed from our life. And I have to accept that. Not everything turns out the way we plan. Not every story has a perfect ending.

"But what about your..." Merek begins, his voice tainted with pain.

"He's dead. There's no use remembering a ghost," I say as my hands find the first ladder rungs. I loop my spear through the small pack I carry, binds snaring, rope clinging tight to the petrified wood. There's only one item I'll never leave behind.

"Hopefully there'll be no more ghosts where we're going," Hearth says.

Merek tries to say something in agreement, but the words are only a gasp.

"Up you go," Hearth says.

And I climb, my arms shivering with each rung, the wood slick from the sweat of all who had come before us. The pain in my arm is immense. I was almost absorbed, autonomy forced into communal un-death. I could feel it there, for a moment, the thoughts of all swarming through that twining tendril, their human and animal voices swimming into my blood, crawling their way through my veins to scream and swear and promise and pray inside my brain. I heard all the hopes and dreams and despair and truth that dwelled in the thousands and thousands of connected skulls, their enjambed tongues carrying over one another until nothing made sense, all sentences one garbled wail, all of it calling me to join in the eternal shriek. Then the spear brought silence, the quiet calm of a singular mind, not the cacophony of all ends.

My father wouldn't speak to me again.

I wouldn't hear his call rising up to me from below.

I couldn't discern his words in the chaos.

He was already gone. What I wouldn't have given to hear a last goodbye, those final phrases he should have spoken on the night he drifted off, but never spoke. Everything is sad, but the constant reminder wasn't fair. Things have to slip forward, past crumbling away, dust to dust and all that.

So I climb and Hearth follows, Merek shoulder slung, the two grunting under the strain. But this is the easiest part, high above the writhing mass, no limb long enough to reach us, no call enticing enough to bring us back down.

We are free.

Only the green canopy looms above, the light warm and inviting, so many promises made, so many promises kept.

25. Hearth

Merek is lighter than my pack. This is a blessing, and a pleasant surprise. He's a big man. Much bulk. The ladder is high and I am so tired. The end is in sight as I watch the thing below wallow and wade over the bag I'd left at the ladder's base. I wonder what we have lost in its contents, what of our past lives won't make it into our new lives. Does it matter? What was worth bringing from one to the next? The less we carry, the less burden we continue to shoulder. We still have the knowledge in our heads, the memories we cherish, those few good moments interspersed with all the suffering. Maybe the amalgams can learn from what's in the pack. Maybe something inside will save them. Maybe they are all too far gone, minds siphoned into that other world, no lasting connection able to bring them back, to make sense of the knickknacks and cooking utensils and framed photographs now in their possession.

As we climb, the scent of flowers and soil and actual breathing life replace the wine-stained rot below. The green light blossoms, the sun's warmth replacing the heated fever-bodies below.

The voices of our friends call in celebration. The beastly wails are swallowed, background noise fading to a dull din. I try not to think of the list. Those names subsumed, the ones who don't get to celebrate above. I hope they died before their bodies welded into one, sinew to sinew. I don't know how much of the blood that coats my skin belonged to them, or to the beast, or if there was any division between the two anymore. Death was inevitable. You pay for what you receive. And we are about to receive so much.

The verdant growth.

The promise of health, of safety, of joy.

Hopefully it was worth it.

It will always be worth it.

26. Watcher

I see them among the trees. I watch as they laugh and gambol and cheer. They embrace. They kiss. They swing loved ones around, tromping through undergrowth, hands clasped, smiles most likely pulling at their faces (our binoculars only see so much). I recognize my neighbors, for a time, then they start to blend, to become distanced, somehow absorbed into the trees, wandering on from the lip of the chasm, becoming one with the forest. Literal or metaphoric, I don't know. So much devours so much. But I know I wouldn't stay close to the thing that caused me pain, if such a thing were an option. But I am planted, my body one with the sagging chair beneath me, my skull having adjusted to the lenses, rubber gaskets becoming a second skin over my eyes.

I am happy for them, but I am also happy for myself. The final sight arrives soon. They get their desired experience. I get mine. So I, too, will be dancing beneath the leafy canopy, hands clasped to theirs, turning and turning and turning with elation. My body isn't strong enough now, but then, then will be a different case. Muscles un-atrophied. Feet no longer shedding bone. I will join all my Watcher brothers and sisters in rebirth. I will be there too.

To watch has been a privilege.

I can feel my heart slow, my lungs sluggish in their intake.

To watch has been a joy.

The thoughts come slower.

To watch may have been an excuse, but we all make excuses, need excuses. No one is infallible, we all know. But the final sight doesn't weigh judgment. The final sight accepts all worshipers at its altar, and I've done nothing but worship.

The trees will belong to us.

Our bodies will feed their roots.

Our blood will wick through their trunks, flourish in leaves.

Our eyes will be forever planted.

Forever seeing.

Hopefully not forever blind.

The Neon Dread of Leaves

by Tiffany Morris

Kudzu choked lilacs with their livid, mutated yellow-green leaves. Metal to vein: their vines writhed in a gasping, hissing susurration when cut. The spores and pollen flung into pores, concrete, every break and crack in a five-mile radius. The air was hazy with the gold dust, sticking and oozing, vomiting in its sweetness.

There was a quiet writhing of plants sighing and stretching green and blooming over the structures that once hummed busy with cash register beeps and screens chirping blue LED light: a time before the verdant insistence of growth, of blossoming. The peace of the cities became the peace of death: its mechanical rhythms of machinery and capital silenced. Mila trudged, one foot in front of the other, trying not to let exhaustion make her pause for too long. Her wife, Greta, led the way, her head high even while traversing the living wasteland, her long dark hair wrapped into a neat bun. Mila didn't know how she did it. Mila had been avoiding mirrors, but she knew the grey of her roots must have been slowly inching downward, fading her looks sunbleached, her skin dry as driftwood. When they'd met five years ago at a coworker's dinner party, Greta and Mila had guessed each other's ages. Mila was great at this–she knew that the tall, sturdy Greta was likely fifty-two, but she guessed forty-five, just to be polite. Greta had snorted in the sort of no-nonsense way that would always, in the years to come, make Mila laugh. Maybe it was the merlot that night—she'd never handled dark wines well—but she had felt giddy, flushed. Greta, for her part, had guessed that Mila was forty-seven and was surprised that Mila was ten years older.

She was grateful for her wife, her strong hands that gently pushed aside the vines and cut them when needed, whenever they encountered a bunch too tangled and thick to pass. The streets were clogged and blooming, every neighborhood now green and seething, splattered in parts with pollen and blood.

Five swallows scattered, startled, from the rain-heavy trees. Mila turned her head sharply in the direction from which they'd fled. She dropped her knife and whetstone with a soft knock. A figure in the distance shambled closer, a human-shaped neon dread of leaves and snapping branches that she couldn't comprehend. A strangled scream escaped her throat. The figure finally took the shape of Greta, stumbling home clumsy-legged and choking, groaning. Mila rushed to her, feet pounding the forest floor with dull staccato thuds, a panicked drumming that matched her heartbeat.

Greta cried and coughed. Her tears were thick with sap, and with each convulsion she choked sap out from her trembling mouth. Jagged shards of bark came out with it. It smelled like fresh evergreen trees: life and death merging into one sickly sweet cloud that smothered the forest.

Greta's full weight collapsed onto her wife. All Mila could do was scream.

———◆———

The plague was of unknown origin: there were symptoms that could lay dormant for weeks before it became infectious and, instantly, too late. The itching skin could be mistaken for hives, the symptoms like any allergy, really, coughing and discomfort on the skin made raw like a woolen sweater left on too long or sweated against or rubbed the wrong way, sweaters like she'd been given at Christmas every year by Greta's Aunt Geri, lovingly knit during her long stretches of sunny solitary afternoons. Aunt Geri had died from the sickness. Greta had insisted on checking on her, had stopped Mila from going into the apartment, but Mila could still smell it, the overpowering sweetness of lavender and the sickly-thick scent of honeysuckle, the low-slung stench of rot and mold that it covered. It got all over her clothes just from standing in the hallway and set itself deep in Mila's sweaty hair as she heard Greta's wail. The ungodly guttural scream was the scream of mourning, and realization carved itself deeply into Mila: Geri, Greta's last living family member, had been overtaken by the thrumming green sickness. Time yawned eternal in the too-hot hallway, the air conditioning long turned off and no longer making the dark stretch of silence habitable. The darkness wrapped its arms around her as she listened to screams dissolve to sobs dissolve to silence. Mila knocked gently on the open doorway. No sounds rustled within. Mila started to step in and then thought better of it. More darkness and silence, dull green glows from open apartments, the vines hissing and writhing over the windowpanes. Greta emerged from the dim apartment. Mila tried to ignore the look on her wife's face. The light was turned off somewhere behind her eyes as they both settled into a new truth: it was just the two of them now.

———

Greta had gone North to see if anyone was left up there, this place where she'd had distant relatives, people who would recognize her on last name alone, and according to Mila's calendar—ragged knife notches on the wall, carved pine sigils—she'd been gone for a month. Mila tried to keep busy, tidying the small site, stopping to take breaks when her body began to ache, or a hot flash tore through her in a lightning-jolt, panic and irritation mixed in the unrelenting heat. She'd sweat and shiver with the cool breeze, the discomfort so intense she pushed out thoughts of death.

It didn't seem fair to have to experience menopause at a time like this.

Greta had told Mila to stay put in their cabin, surrounded by thickets of pine trees and a small brown brook, its babbling the only comforting constant Mila knew. They'd barely ever used this place for vacations. Mila laughed, harsh, bitter. They'd never get vacations again.

She'd be fine, Greta had insisted, voice calm and firm over Mila's sobbing. Greta had always been the brave one, the one who could assess a situation with detached resolve, the one to know the best route forward. Finding Geri had been the only time that Mila had ever seen her crack, her wife so strong and resolute even when the cities had started to fall into their uncanny green silences.

"You know the land," Greta had pointed out to her. "Remember what you were taught."

It was true; Mila had known ever since she was a child how to purify the water and forage plants and mushrooms, had known that these beings carried their own life and wisdom, and she'd wondered about them any time she walked through the woods, wishing she could speak their many different languages. Mila hoped she could call on that knowledge, if needed, but it was hard to remember her own power without Greta and her encouragement. Mila had even been a perfect shot at one point but she hadn't had to hunt anything in years. A shotgun leaned lazily by the cabin bed; a box of shells was stuck somewhere underneath it. It was just in case the canned food ran out, she reassured herself. A few rabbits, maybe a deer, nothing bigger than that would trample down the small path to the cabin. No bears, no moose, none of the infected. She said it to herself like a mantra, like a prayer.

———◦———

Greta stared at her wife's face, contorted in pain.

"Greta?!" Mila cried, cradling her body. "What can I do?"

Greta closed her eyes and sap pasted over them: a lock stuck latched. Mila tried to pry them open but couldn't and didn't push. She didn't want to injure her.

Mila stood and tried to pull Greta to her feet, but Greta's full, slack weight was too much for her. Greta's nostrils were covered, her mouth was closing, and she knew Greta would choke again. Mila kept trying to stick her fingers into her mouth to keep it open, to keep the sap from pasting it closed, too. Her fingers became stained with the thick sweet sap that stank and stung as it entered her wounds and smothered her wife.

When Greta died, who knows how much longer it had been, she closed her mouth and Mila could not open it. Mila ran screaming inside the cabin and locked the door—to keep her safe from what?—and cried, hands fumbling toward the shelf, she needed a slug of whiskey to get her through this and the bottle shook in her hands and kept shaking as the liquor burned its way down her throat.

The insistent thrum of the rain buried itself in her brain and oh God she'd have to bury Greta, bury her in the mud at some point, who knew if Greta had found anything or if the world was just empty now, just Mila and the hissing rain that wouldn't stop and the plague that came crawling for everyone, choking them from the inside out. She didn't know what to do. She had lost everyone but Greta before the plague had even started—horrible year after horrible year of loss, her few friends, her small family. Greta had experienced similar losses—suicides and cancer and old age—and finding each other had been a miracle. Now it would just be her. The thought repeated in her head, a chant, a curse. Just her, just her—

She screamed and didn't know when she would stop. She would be alone in this cabin, with just the brook, waiting for the infected to come, waiting for the vines to wrap around her in their embrace and pull her into their depths of unknowing, of whatever hell realm was below the Earth that it devoured.

Light was draining outside the cabin when Mila's eyes, sore from crying, locked on the shotgun. She stumbled toward it, drunk, blurred at the edges with blue-hot rage. She loaded the gun, fingers numb and clumsy. Could she do this? With the weight of the gun the world made sense again, a calm settled itself somewhere between her eyes and she knew she could end it, there was nothing left, no world out there, no cure, not a soul in sight, no one she knew to get through this with her. She held it in her mouth and tasted the metal, hands still shaking, everything heavy and dark like sleep. She willed her hands to do the work.

They wouldn't.

The rain continued to thrum on the roof. Mila set the gun down gently on the bed and walked back out into the forest, where her wife's body laid, buzzing, humming from within. She approached Greta, a shiver trembling its way through her bones as she found her wife's body already wrapped in buds and leaves. Vines hissed and stretched in the trees around her. Mila kneeled and cradled the leaf-strewn head in her hands. Somewhere beneath the devouring green was Greta's skin, her face, the place where her thoughts had lived and her eyes that once had been open and would stare into hers, gleaming in the light of morning.

The buds on the leaves were almost ready to bloom. The stretching and sighing of life snaked its way around Greta's otherwise unmoving body. The blossoms would open and hiss and screech silent, sending a cloud of pollen into the air again. Mila sobbed, her clenched-shut eyes still swollen and bleary from the exhausted tears that had marked every hour of the accursed, wretched day.

Then the rustling started from beneath Greta's skin. Mila heard it first in a soft scratch, beneath the gentle rain and the hiss and screech of vine and bloom, she heard a buzz and rustle from the heap that had once entombed her wife. The buzz grew louder. A chasm—what had been Greta's mouth—burst open, too wide, too yawning, a scream unending as leaves crawled out and wrapped around her skull. Seeds vomited out of Greta's mouth, wet pink petals and gleaming yellow capsules, sticky pulp and pistil. Flying ants clattered out, a whole colony of them, the roar of their wings and legs deafening like the sound of hell and Mila could only cry. Exhaustion prevented her from screaming. Her reason for being here, her tether to this world that had once carried so many people, so much noise and beauty and distraction, was lost forever in this verdant horror, this life insistent on its new forms. She did not move to avoid them. This land that she'd once known how to traverse, this world that had been familiar to her, was transforming all the time, was moving beyond the reaches of her understanding. She had been prepared for the world to change, it had so often seemed to move on without her as she lost time to grief, but this was something too monstrous, too determined to devour her in its hungry jaws, and now, much too strong for her to keep resisting.

The yellow-green spores danced in the dim light, their neon glimmer careening fast toward   her and Mila remained stuck in place and sank deeper into the mud and pine needles. She closed her eyes as the ants landed on her, each of them biting into her flesh, sticking the sick pollen into her, wounds clotting instantly with thick sap. She opened her mouth and the air was honey and the ants hummed inside and scratched themselves against the walls of her lungs. She choked and gasped and the sap started to pool, but she knew she would breathe in a new way soon, drinking in sunlight, her skin hard with bark or soft with the glue smell of the white ichor in her veins. An ecstasy washed like golden light over her as the sun finally broke through the clouds and she could hear them, the heartbeat and whispers of everyone who had died, Greta and Geri singing welcome in their new language, the soft green and gold petalbright and transmuting light into breath, she felt one last jolt of joy as she realized she would soon be light as air and smell like lavender and honeysuckle, speaking the language of plant and tree and the verdant root system that carried life through the whole teeming world. Vines pulsed into her body as breath mixed with light and sprayed pollen into the air, the pain exquisite as the green tore through her flesh threading through her pores now blooming bright roselike flowers that would smother her old, outmoded, too-human despair. Soon it would all be light and buzzing and new: all she had to do was stand there and be swallowed by the beauty of what she was becoming.

A New and Different Hunger

by Tiffany Morris

There were so many ways to scream. Blood-curdling: deep, immense, primal, rumbling up from the gut. Yelping: fear swallowing itself and spitting back up. A screech: like an eagle, like its prey. A cry: surprise, tears, startled softness.

All of those screams were coming from the field.

A cabin: a mile from the beach. Sighing shoreline. Tall grasses. Plenty of tree cover. If you'd taken a helicopter over it, you'd have seen a jagged, snakelike coast, water coiling and biting at the rocks. The coast eroded and evaporated. Displaced creatures kept moving inland. The homes hadn't moved—they were safe for the moment.

That's where she'd first found them. A mile from the beach, her own backyard. A field of silhouettes in the fog. Silhouettes that she knew: graceful, unworldly, powerful.

Horses.

She hadn't wanted to approach; too much risk of spooking them. She knew that from her childhood, from the summer she'd spent on Aunt Jo's farm.

She stood, silent, still.

Yes, she knew horses, Aunt Jo had owned five of them: Appaloosa, Falabella, breeds with exotic-sounding names. Aunt Jo's living room was filled with horse-racing trophies and ribbons, gold galloping figurines. It was a world shinier than the bottom of a beer can.

Erin had loved being on that farm, even though it sweltered in the heat and everything stank. It was staggeringly alive: there were wildflowers and bees and hissing barn cats, mean and fat on the bodies of field mice. At night, the barking of coyotes filled the sky.

"They've made their kill," Aunt Jo would say, a smile spread across her face.

Erin spent her days with Aunt Jo, tending to the horses, marvelling at how her tiny aunt handled the rough work of the farm. Aunt Jo was like no one Erin had ever seen: ropey muscle and scraggly brown hair flecked with grey. Sunken eyes. Her face was unworldly and beautiful, betraying her unknown origins: Aunt Jo had just turned up beside the river behind the family's farm, something red and bloodied in the water, her clothes tattered and teeth chattering.

"The poor thing couldn't even speak," her mother had said. "We took her in and let the police know, but no one had ever reported her missing. So, you know, she just became one of us.

Things were different then, of course. She would've ended up in the system if it happened now."

Erin knew, of course, that that wasn't the whole story. Aunt Jo had told her that she no memory of where she'd come from, had been prone to night terrors and sleepwalking and disappearing into the inkdark river where the family had found her. She would leave wet and muddied bare footprints from the front step up to her room, scowling as she scrubbed them down when she awakened. Erin, too, was a sleepwalker, though she never seemed to leave the house: she'd wake suddenly, most often at the back door, with no memory of dream or how she had gotten there. The family kept five locks on the door, just in case, armed only before the house went dark with sleep. Jo understood this mystery affliction, how the dark became a craving so strong your body would move without you knowing, waking.

After that summer on the farm, leaves sighed and stretched their golden haze over the world and Erin mournfully returned to the city, to school, to a world of homework and bullies and bus routes. The world outside the farm was alien to her, hostile and strange, a place full of unspoken tests she always seemed to fail.

"Don't worry about those people," Jo had told her. "Just be yourself and it'll work out in the end."

Erin wasn't so sure. Every year the schoolroom was full of tests, written and unwritten. She would say the wrong thing to people and her classmates would roll their eyes at her, calling her names, mocking her tallness, her awkward clumsiness. Solitude, she realized, was something much more comforting, something she could choose.

Her mother had returned one night from Aunt Jo's, her voice full of tears and face drawn. Erin sat outside the locked bedroom door and waited for a signal, listened for a return to calm. Her mother's sobs were interspersed with the croaked snippets of a phone conversation: *unidentified, entrails, disappeared.* Erin had known what *presumed drowned* meant: the river had finally taken Jo back.

When they'd gone to the farm to pack up her stuff, most traces of Jo had already vanished. Erin stood at the door of the barn, hesitant, stomach clenched. She tried to steady her breath, inhaling, counting to three, before she went in. The cats had fled. The horses were long gone, the stable silent without them. She peered into one of the stalls. The hay was trampled with hoof prints and matted with pools of dried blood. When she walked down to the river, the sun was slung low on the horizon, and the metallic tang of death writhed in the steady, trickling water.

When Erin stood in that field outside her cabin, the night full of billowing fog and those graceful grazing silhouettes, she wasn't at all surprised to hear Aunt Jo's voice.

"Look at them," Aunt Jo crooned. "Look at those lovely horses."

Erin hoped the horses would come back in the daylight, where she could be easily seen and, hopefully, be approached by the creatures. She carried a sandwich bag filled with corn kernels, apple slices, anything to coax the horses to her—for her part, all she was craving lately was meat. Better to give them some of the stuff she wasn't eating before it went to waste.

She walked along the field, crows circling overhead. She walked through the field and through the trees until she hit the empty shore, where the grey waves broke hard against the large, jagged boulders. There were no farms for miles. That was what she'd liked about it there. The solitude of the country felt much better than the alienation of towns and cities.

Infinity hummed and sang in the rhythmic crash. The beach stayed empty the whole time she was there, grey on slate on stone. The humid summer air was silver and stinging. She thought again of Aunt Jo, and how similar they'd been: adoptees with somnambulism, odd folks with an intense draw to the water. Missing her aunt was a sharp ache in her side: who knew what kind of person she might have become if she'd grown up with Jo's company, her influence and empathy.

She left the desolate beach, savoring the dull sunlight as it beat down upon her face.

———◦———

Erin drank the last of her glass of wine and placed her dishes in the sink, gazing out the window. With nightfall the horses might have returned.

She grabbed the bag of apples and corn from the fridge and enjoyed its coolness against her skin, ignoring the nausea the fresh food evoked in her. Taking the flashlight from the counter, she slid the screen door open and walked out into the dark yard. She made her way to the field, where silhouettes bowed and neighed in the deepening haze of night. The spring peepers started and stopped in unison with each step she took. The silence was a breeze breaking through the dark.

Her heart leapt as she moved closer to the horses. The silhouettes stopped and turned to her. The smell of blood carried thick in the humid air. Her stomach clenched. Were they injured?

One silhouette was lying on its side. Erin shone her flashlight over to it. A deep redblack pool soaked into the bleached grass. She moved the light up. The beam was clinical and bright against the wet intestines spilling from the carcass, its splayed-open abdomen.

Erin screamed and stumbled backward. Her hand reached out and hit the side of a horse, its fur sticky and matted with blood. Her hand rolled over its emaciated frame, the jutting bones poking out from under its skin.

This wasn't right.

Horses mourned their dead.

She turned around and stepped back again, shining her light on the horse she'd stumbled into. Its massive black eyes gleamed lantern-bright in the flashlight. It snorted, impassive, its face drenched in blood.

The horses were devouring the carcass.

Erin dropped the bag. Her screaming chased her back into the house.

———◦———

Dim daylight crept between the fingers of the cabin window blinds. Erin had slept a fitful sleep, cut-through with images of carcasses flayed open, maggots and rot churning within them.

She fumbled through breakfast, unsure of whether she should check the field in daytime. What if they were still there? The yolk of her eggs smeared across her plate. The greasy smell filled her nostrils and her stomach jumped into her throat in revulsion. She was ravenous and nauseated all at once. Maybe some bacon, later. Maybe some raw steak. Erin conjured the images and didn't feel her stomach flip-flop. An encouraging sign. But for now, breakfast had been a waste; she scraped the remnants into the garbage and did the dishes, squinting out the window. She couldn't see the horses.

Erin put on her boots and, with unsteady feet, made her way to the field.

It was empty. No birds sang there. All was stillness and stifling silence. Sweat beaded on her lower back. The grass faintly trampled, faintly stained, smelled sweet and rotten.

With nightfall the horses might come again. In the field, in the dark, they'd lie in wait.

———◦———

Five nights passed, and she hadn't dared go into the field. Erin conjured the images of the horses in her mind readily; each time, fear transformed into guilt. Their food sources must have been dwindling if they'd resorted to cannibalism. Their jutting bones writhed and shifted in her memories.

Maybe they just needed different food. She could give them some of her supply. Erin ate a last forkful of rare steak. She savored the blood on her tongue before swallowing. Horses didn't usually eat meat, but maybe these ones had developed a taste for it. Her own hunger for meat had grown insatiable; she'd stocked up, filling her grocery cart with foam package after foam package screaming bright red in the fluorescent supermarket light.

There was plenty to go around.

Night fell and she went back to the field. Raw, bloody hamburger seeped through the plastic wrap of the package and onto her hands. She resisted the urge to take a small handful and let it dissolve on her tongue. The sodden Styrofoam tray left a trail from the house to the field.

The skeletal silhouettes were already there.

"Hi," Erin said, her voice shaky. She reached out a tentative hand to pat one of the horses. Its thin frame was a word spoken into wind.

She took a wet clump of meat from the package and held it out to the horse.

A clamor of neighing came from the creatures. They did not take the food. Erin set down the package and stood, helpless. What did they want?

She caught her reflection in the horse's void-black eye. Aunt Jo's face smiled back at her.

These creatures had a new and different hunger.

One of the horses began walking in the direction of the water. Its eyes glowed red when caught in her flashlight. She knew she had to follow it, to see where it had come from. As she took unsteady steps behind it, the other horses stayed still and disappeared into shadow. Erin kept the bluewhite beam of the light trained in front of her as she followed the horse to the shore.

The water grew louder. Under it, the faint sound of screaming erupted staccato from some distant field. It eventually gurgled into silence. Then there was only water once again.

A sliver of waning moon glinted softly on the crashing waves. The horse ran from her sight: a pounding sound as it dissolved into the ocean. Panic ran through Erin's legs as she froze in place, fruitlessly moving the beam over the shoreline, looking for the strange creature.

Something was moving in the water. Erin squinted into the blackened horizon, moving her flashlight over the churning waves, the hiss and crash of the charcoal and oyster rhythm pounding against the rocks. Indiscernible shadows moved inside shadow as her heart crashed erratic in her chest, a strange dread and longing surging together as she took dizzied breaths.

Something made her want to run into it headlong, to disappear into the dark cold water.

She stepped forward, her shoes soaking in the freezing surf.

Another dizzied breath.

A surging roar thundered around her as a herd of horses emerged from the ocean, hissing and screeching, running forward in shadows and moonlight, lines of scales glinting beneath their tufts of fur. Erin dropped her flashlight and screamed, her legs finally propelling her into motion.

Her feet stumbled over rock and sand as her seaweed hair bounced and danced in the wind. Her spine bent and shifted in agony as her bones thickened under stretching, itching, burning skin. Iridescent scales sprouted out of her flesh as she fell to her knees and found herself not stopped but running, her new black eyes watching the foam break against rock as her kelpie skin absorbed the light.

She could taste the blood waiting for her. She ran into the field, staggeringly alive with want. Her new form was a memory of hunger, and a promise, finally, of home.

The Honey Harvest
by Tiffany Morris

Golden dappled light sang through the hot air of September, thick with the last sighs of summer. George took deep breaths, drinking the deep honeyed scent as he readied the harvest. Bees droned and danced lazy arcs in the air, the apiary his home within their home.

It was the time of the second reaping. Some of the bees landed and crawled over him, their gentle bodies curious in their movements over the protective cover of his white canvas coat. He talked to them, his voice muffled by the straw mask that enclosed his face.

No one at the farm knew that he loved talking to the bees. This swarm had heard so many of his hopes, fears, confessions, murmured from behind his strange faceless visage. He was certain that they knew him—he remembered hearing that bees knew faces—and if they knew faces, surely they'd know his gait, voice, movements, familiar as he'd become over the past few weeks.

It was better, easier, really, to talk with them than it was with people. He didn't stutter with them like he did with other people, especially Ezekiel, whose stern face and solemn pronouncements would embarrass George, make his cheeks flush apple-red whenever his steely gaze fell on him. Ezekiel, with his commanding presence, could make anyone feel like they were the only person in the room. The women murmured about it all the time, in glowing voices of hushed excitement, themselves flushed apple-red. George hated his tendency to blush as much as he hated his stutter. He was a grown man of thirty-five with the expressions of an awkward teenaged boy, fumbling his way through life, feeling like he'd grown up feral. His parents had been neglectful, spiteful people, as quick with a cruel barb as they were with a beating, but they'd at least taught him how to talk—if only he could show it.

When Ezekiel's eyes held him, it stirred a mix of fear and fascination in his gut. Even through clenched fists, Ezekiel was beautiful, had the kind of gaze that made you want to be loved by him.

Still, George wondered, did the bees know Ezekiel's face?

Ezekiel was the reason he'd ended up working the hives in the first place—an attempt to punish him with what was, usually, women's work, punishment for getting caught making little sculptures from grass, hay, sticks. He left them out on the outer edge of the Redthistle Farm property, by the barbed-wire fence line, where no one else really bothered to go. They were small crude shapes of faceless people, a few animals, one deer with bristling branch antlers, of which he'd been particularly proud. As Ezekiel glared at him, he'd reminded him that this sort of thing was foolish, pointless, for only God could create the truly new. Then he crumpled the figures in his large fists like so much aged paper.

George had taken to the apiary labors easily, but still made sure to grumble about it from time to time, so that no one knew how much he liked it. Loving this work, after all, might seem like defiance, or worse, deviance.

As he pulled it out, the comb was a deep red, the hexagonal structure brimming with sanguine sweetness. The blood-orange of the honey was distinctive enough to create demand in the neighboring communities, and the honey helped the ministry stay afloat. The red thistles that gave the farm its name grew sentinel-straight in a patch along the western side of the property, and the bees waltzed daily within the flowers.

"You don't want to go to town and sell the honey, trust me," Marita, Ezekiel's first wife, said. "It's far too much on the senses. Plus, people gawk at you." George nodded. He probably wouldn't turn down the opportunity if it ever presented itself, but it hardly felt urgent. His life before the farm had been empty, quiet, lonely: a haze of cubicle anonymity and a barely-furnished apartment, microwave meals, doldrums and dullness. It was fate that he'd discovered the honey, then the farm, then his salvation. He never missed the outside world, reduced to a passing curiosity as time went on. The farm was beautiful, simple, meaningful to him, and any price to stay there was worth it.

———————

In the morning there was Hank, and the faded silhouette of his body that sweated through his memory and onto his mattress. A ghost.

George stayed with the apparition. It had to be the faint scent of the honey stuck to him, or the smell had come in through the window, left slightly ajar to let the coolness in overnight. He breathed deeply. The air held that smell, that honey-mixed-with-skin scent that was, still, just Hank, who had also gladly worked the apiary when he'd been punished.

"We could be perfect anywhere," Hank said, his beautiful dark eyes flinted with fool's gold in the sunlight. "I don't think it has to be here."

George hadn't said anything.

"I don't think we'll ever get Ezekiel to approve of this," Hank added. "And this is important to me."

Hank had threaded his fingers through George's own, their palms fitting together in soft symmetry.

George took another deep breath. The smell readily conjured the feeling of stubble, kissing and burning his face. Hank's farm-strengthened hands, his reassurances, his patience that made George lose his stutter. Then, of course, the memory of the night they were supposed to escape together. The dogs had been unleashed, but Hank, who could run fast as wind, managed to leave without George who had hesitated too long by the door, whose name was whispered by Hank and then punctured by the dreadful seconds of realization before George heard his lover's running footsteps, George who'd had an excuse ready for anyone who might find him out of bed and in the field, if he had just managed to step beyond the threshold—like a wedding night inverted—

Shame flushed with the already-rising heat of the morning and George drank deeply of the room-temperature water on his nightstand. This was a new day, one that stretched further from that night, and eventually, time's mercy would exorcise Hank from his memory, how Hank had first told him about the bees remembering faces, how they had sneaked their first kiss in the just-faded daylight of the blue hour when beings became shadow. This was when they would meet and it became the hour he loved best. The world was hushing itself but still alive, like George the forever-flushed shadow, blushing and stuttering but alive, blooming there even in the dark.

When the morning had come, no one looked for his long-gone lover.

"People are free to leave," Ezekiel had said at the breakfast table, and he looked directly at George when he said it. George had a feeling that wasn't completely true, given the dogs running out after Hank, but George still blushed and gave him an unsteady nod. He turned back to his blackened toast and took a bite so big he almost choked.

He was telling the bees about seeing a ghost—or, rather, feeling one—when a small, delicate hand brushed George's shoulder and made him jump.

"George?"

It was Pauline, Marita's eldest daughter. She was, if he recalled correctly, 19 years old. She had a thin, nervous face, and pale hair that almost matched her skin, a quiet voice. She was his second ghost of the day.

"Y-y-ou startled me," he said.

"I'm sorry, I can't hear you," she said, gesturing to his mask.

He took it off, suddenly keenly aware of his sweat-soaked hair. His perspiration dripped in rivulets down his back. He resisted the urge to shake it off. Ezekiel's figure stood several yards back, by the workshop, watching the conversation.

"How c-can I help you?"

"My father," she said. "He wants us to get married."

Her face was blank, resigned. He tried not to show the panic that rumbled through him, thunderstorm-close to his skin.

"Oh," he swallowed. "Did-did he get you to come tell me that?"

"No," she laughed nervously. "I'm supposed to flirt with you, to get you to court me. But I'd rather just say it plainly. We both know how it ends up."

"Oh," he said again. A pause. "I s-suppose we do."

She was so young to his thirty-five years, but that wasn't out of the norm at the farm. Even Hank had been ten years younger, but had seemed so much wiser than this girl. And to be married even younger than twenty... it just didn't seem right to him. His dread mixed with pity as he looked at the small gleam of hope in her own grey eyes. They were like her father's, but softer. They did not make you want to beg for love.

"I-I would be honoured to court you," he finally said, the words a vice around his throat. Somewhere in the back of his mind, a rustling recollection of his father's hands crushing against his larynx. He wrapped her frail body in a light hug. He tried not to look in the direction of Ezekiel's silhouette.

———

In the evening, later in the week, when the sunset blazed orange and then gave way to deepening blue, George walked Pauline back to the women's quarters, the lit metal lantern casting their strange shadows on the wooden siding. He pushed down a shudder as her lips brushed his, gentle and dry, feeling the warmth of her hand in his and being forced into the heaviness of her soap scent. All week he had tried not to feel repulsed by her quietness, her tiny body, her wrongness. It wasn't Pauline's fault. She would make a fine wife for anyone, it was just—well, she wasn't Hank, for one, and for another, this coupling surely meant his apiary punishment was near its end. Once married, he could be kept in check by his wife. He was, in the end, being blessed with a beautiful and uncomplicated woman for his deference. For his cowardice.

A surge of rage flowed upward from some deep part of himself, volcanic in its quickness and fury, and he flushed and stumbled backward. Pauline looked at him, confusion apparent even in the low light.

"I-I'm mighty sorry," he said. "I have to keep my p-p-passions in check."

When she giggled coquettishly and said goodnight, voice tinged with an overwrought sultriness, he suppressed the urge to split her head open with an axe.

Instead, George walked over to the apiary, furious tears a vellum on his tanned face. It didn't matter that he wasn't wearing his protective gear, and he didn't care who saw him—there were probably other women that had heard his remark about his passions and assumed he was walking around to cool off.

"This is my face," he said to the bees, holding up the lantern close enough to feel its heat on his cheek, and he whispered to them, his voice barely audible, everything he remembered about Hank.

***

The beautiful blood of the honeycomb made for strange wombwater. He was at the edge of the field, barely visible in the moonlight, sculpting small figures once again. The wax he'd started confiscating held things together with gluelike strength, melting in the daylight and re-solidifying at the colder edges of the evening.

His husband watched him. Well, his sort-of husband, the one he'd sculpted, a grassy figure, decorated with small flowers—buttercups for eyes, a few thistles for hair, a carved honeycomb mouth that tasted sweet. He talked to him, now, instead of the bees. He did not stutter. It had been the bees that gave him this idea, had led him back with an insistent hum to a more hidden edge of the field, a place where trees wrapped their arms around a ramshackle shed long abandoned, where a small patch of red thistles bloomed.

He also talked to this figure instead of Pauline, his betrothed, his false beloved. It made it easier to be with her, to withstand his fate. With this, he could still forge a life he loved here on the farm, the life he had longed for, and he could still win Ezekiel's grace. Pauline, for her part, had seemed more cheerful and less taken by moments of uncertainty since he'd started on this project.

"We can be perfect here," he whispered to the effigy, and the breeze made it rustle slightly, a barely-perceptible nod. He smiled at his husband—he hadn't yet settled on a name, had hoped one evening inspiration would strike and that would be the figure's own way of speaking—when a snap of footfalls fell behind him. He hushed into a deep, panicked quiet.

"Who's there?" Ezekiel's voice asked, eerie in its calm authority.

George willed the entire world into stillness. Perhaps he'd fallen asleep, was dreaming this whole thing—though that would also imperil him.

"I know someone is there," Ezekiel repeated, moving closer.

With a panicked scan of his dark surroundings, George spotted a pile of jagged wood that had long-ago fallen or been chewed off from the shack by some animal. If Ezekiel tried to beat him again, maybe he could use it in defense, somehow—

Or maybe George would deserve the punishment. He fought the confusion rolling like fog through his mind, the thrum of his heart burning into excitement and rage and something murderous that lurked deep behind his fear, and when Ezekiel turned on his lantern and called his name, George stood up soundless and defiant. Ezekiel set down the lantern and wordlessly began to rain his fists on George's body, George's body so cold with sweat and the evening air, and he knocked George down and started pummeling his back. George begged him to stop, tears flowing readily, which made Ezekiel's large fists pound harder, bruises surely blossoming on George's flesh with each wallop.

George told Ezekiel he loved him and would do anything to stay in his grace and Ezekiel moved his hands to George's throat, muttering for him to shut up. Night surrounded him, the shadow of death closing in as air didn't come, but then Ezekiel loosened his grip, and George, by pure instinct, managed to wriggle free, disoriented, rolling over, gasping. Ezekiel stood and George could hear him loosening his belt with a small metal click. He knew he would be whipped with the belt—he had experienced it with his father and George had seen it happen on the farm before, mostly to women—and with a swift jolt of adrenaline George crawled over to the jagged piece of wood and grabbed it. Ezekiel snapped his belt as George pulled himself up and jabbed the sharp wood into Ezekiel's chest, a wooden stake into a vampire, and Ezekiel stumbled backwards into the thistles, a choked wet sound mixing with the snap of the sharp leaves and thorns that took his blood as sacrifice.

George laughed and cried, waiting for the sound of dogs, of confused, worried voices, but the whole farm was quiet. The fight had taken place so far away from the sleeping quarters that none of the grunting, crying, speech, or death had registered. A miracle, he thought absurdly, and George gathered his breath, walked over to the still-burning light, and blew out the lantern.

With quiet steps he walked, carrying his husband, past the bleeding thistles and into the field, past the front gate that he opened and closed easily. Had someone forgotten to lock it? Had it ever really been locked?

He walked softly on the dirt road, carrying his crumbling sculptures in his arms, remembering that the path would lead eventually to pavement, cars, the noise of such different lives than the one he'd been living. He would find love and they could live in the country somewhere else and he could bury this beautiful effigy: 'til death do they part. He held Hank's memory in his heart, making it into a lantern burning without light. A swarm of bees flew alongside him until they tired and the road to the farm shrank to nothing in the horizon behind him.

Looking for the Flower-Man

by Tiffany Morris

A sea littered with shipwrecks, a burning horizon. Black bulbs bloom from white earth: a field, a pile of salt. The flowers quiver in the dull light of a burned-out sun. They hold secrets, medicines, burning truth that can't be held in the blood.

Every day the Flower-Man carries the bouquets in a large wicker basket on his back, bundles wrapped in tongue-red ribbon. He wanders fallow fields, holding onto the promise of blooming. His skull is stained pink with botanical ichor. His clothes smell of pollen, and his voice is the humming of bees. He walks past a hare escaped from a trap; tracking mud, it leaps over a meagre fox corpse. The fur is not enough for a pelt. A magpie flies in the grey stratosphere. It tracks the townspeople and carries messages to the Devil.

You do not know what disaster transformed this town into ruin. It rusts at the borders. It dissolves, it erodes, it falls apart. Mouths stretch to scream and the sky stretches with them. Light refracts on the busy parks. The people gather there, at the banks of the river, and they do not know what they are looking for; they do not know where they are looking. They watch as the water vomits oil rainbows and thick sludge that bubbles over the banks.

You pass two men covered in shining scales. They weep. They hold hands. They kiss in the light, gold and red, their devotion enduring. Love weaves ivy garlands through their hair. The rot of ruin transforms or enhances the human condition, who knows, the weather has never been predictable. You cannot decide how you feel about this new collapsing world, other than lonely, that much is certain, but even in this devastated place the windows stay open, curtains flutter accordingly.

A woman on a bench lives seven stages of life at once. They flicker out ghostly from her, extending at each side. When she breathes in, they collapse into her single self, in her middle age. The grey locks of her old woman hair fly wild, snakelike, around her. Her smile cracks and trembles at the corners.

You tell her you are looking for the Flower-Man. "Have you seen him today?" you ask her.

Her seven selves shake their heads no. Only some of them are smiling.

"I'll try the bakery," you say. Five sets of shoulders shrug, two remain motionless.

The bakery has stayed open, despite it all. The windows are boarded up and strange scenes are painted on the wood: goblins and swans eating ripe oranges. The inside of the store is bright and smells of spun sugar and heavy whipping cream. Cakes shine in chrome and glass display cases. Small vestiges of a once-life.

The weary young man at the counter doesn't look up.

"Excuse me, do you use flower essences?"

"I don't work here," he says. He drops coins on the counter but doesn't move to leave. He has a scar running along his cheek.

"Oh. Well." A pause. "Have you seen the Flower-Man?" you ask.

"He's in the cemetery today," he replies. He finally looks at you and smiles. His scar stretches his skin. "It's migration day."

"Of course!" You'd forgotten. "I'll have to get there right away."

"I'm headed there myself. I never like to miss it."

"Are you waiting for anyone?"

He ignores the question and moves out from behind the counter. He gestures for you to follow him and you walk along his right side, back into the town now bustling. The light feels different as you walk, the day spitting golden as you both move into a cemetery procession. The people dance and shuffle and march around you, weeping and laughing. A violin player moves among the crowd. A purple and orange sound vibrates from the instrument, making you feel warm. It feels just how the bakery smelled.

The cemetery yawns quiet into the edge of town. The grass was soft and green there, once, but now it shines metallic. Still, it is peaceful, and on migration days, people wait for the spirits of the dead to return and perch in the trees: birds with spectral plumage.

"Oh, I don't have an offering," you tell the young man. You only have the money for the flowers. He reaches into his pocket and gives you an old arcade coin. It is a dull, fake gold.

"Don't worry," the young man says. "I use these every year. They're rare, from the before time."

"Thank you."

"I wouldn't want anyone to miss it," he says. "It's my favorite day."

"I hear it's always a good time," you reply. You can't remember the last time you were in the cemetery for migration day—a blessing of loneliness, where everyone disappeared instead of dying. It wasn't for a lack of loss—even people with all-living relatives had ancestors who remember the descendants to come in the afterlife–but you also have faint memories of hating the spectacle, the gawking, the strangeness of the Flower-Man and the chasm of his empty eyes.

The cemetery gates stretch wrought iron arms around the graves. Fresh blooms from the Flower-Man mark each one, pink and orange and yellow and white gleaming against epitaphs so that the spirits may feel welcomed and respected.

At the entrance, a man with gold teeth takes the arcade coin from your outstretched hand. For maintenance, God Bless, he says to each person as they enter.

You follow the young man to a large sycamore tree. The first thing to appear on the tree limb is a leg, then a torso, arms, a skull. Skin. A smiling mouth and eyes that look everywhere and nowhere, all at once.

"Welcome back," the young man says to the spirit. He reaches into his pocket and leaves a crumpled daisy at the bottom of the tree. The spirit continues to smile.

"Do you know him?" you ask.

"No, but my Uncle should arrive sometime today. I have a special coin for him."

Before you can ask to see it, he says, "I am going to go look for him now. I'll see you later."

"Thank you again," you reply, but the young man has already set on his way to the northern part of the grounds. An electricity, thunderstorm-vivid, crackles in the air and you don't resist the small smile stretching your mouth. Your fatigue lessens as you walk among the strewn flowers and candies and letters. An arm, a leg, a torso, a grinning skull: the spirits come to roost in the tall, reaching limbs, mouthing mute greetings to the world of the living, flickering gaslamp beautiful against sighing leaves.

You spot the Flower-Man. He approaches you, hunched over but whistling his honeyed humming. There are only two bouquets left: one of prim bright narcissus and one of the poison black bulbs. The bulbs are the dripping promise of death. They are your writhing, rotting, hissing desire, to join the court of preening ghosts, to leave the world of perpetual collapse. Bees fly out from the Flower-Man's empty eye sockets and crawl along his pink skull, where flesh had once stretched over him.

The magpie is chased out of the cemetery by laughing spirits. Something in your chest breaks open, a flood of light and promise.

"A bouquet of narcissus, please," you finally say, placing the last of your coins in his skeletal hand.

There would be time yet for poisons and their tearing of the veil. There was, for now, this day of spun sugar, an open window, a fluttering curtain caught in the wind that carries the dead home.

On Phantom Wings
by Eric Raglin

Chapter 1

Gael hadn't expected to reunite with Maya for one final birding trip. He could count on one hand the number of times they'd talked, mostly through texts, since their last one five years back. A "happy birthday!" here and a "did you hear ____ died?" there, but little more. Their friendship had grown distant in the rearview as adult life sped forward.

But unexpectedly, the rhythms of their lives aligned one summer.

June stretched out before Gael, lonesome and stifling. Unexpectedly out of a job and with too much time to think, he spent hours pacing in front of his AC window unit, his mind drifting to Maya. They'd been best friends through their early twenties, never going a day without attending an Earth Unity Alliance meeting together, gossiping on the phone, or dancing the night away at their favorite gay bar. Why had Gael let that connection fade? Maybe it wasn't too late to save it. To water a withered plant and bring it back to green glory.

He deleted his message to Maya a half dozen times before he settled on something both awkward and apologetic: *Hey, I know it's been forever and I've been bad at reaching out, but if it's not too weird, want to go on another birding trip? A few days in the forest would heal my soul, haha.*

Maya's response arrived within seconds: *Holy shit, yes, please.*

Quickly, they settled on their location: one of the last stretches of old-growth forest in the state. This area wasn't subject to park status protection, and Gael and Maya weren't even sure it was open to the public. But when adventure called, they answered.

On a Saturday morning, Gael drove to pick up Maya, her house only ten minutes away. Given how close they lived to each other, it was a wonder they hadn't hung out even once over the past five years. With a little planning and effort, they could have gotten together for a bar trivia night, an evening walk around the lake, or a spring concert at the outdoor amphitheater. Gael tried not to blame himself. All that mattered was the work he was doing to nourish the friendship now, perhaps even keeping it alive beyond just this trip.

Maya hadn't had a vacation in ages; her job at Songbird Stewards kept her too busy. After the last day she took off, she'd needed a full week to catch back up. In that time, Maya's boss gave her countless disappointed looks, as if Maya were the team's weak link. Such was the environment of this progressive nonprofit.

Maya imagined how her boss would look at her when she returned from this four-day birding trip: eyes wide and twitching, smile tense. "How was it, Maya?" she would ask. "Relaxing enough for you?"

Even thinking about this possibility roiled Maya's gut, but she tried to tamp down the feeling. If only she could quit the job for good. Stop spending sixty hours a week catering to rich donors who cared more about feeling like saints than actually saving birds.

Squeezing boxes of protein bars into her nearly full backpack, Maya ran a mental checklist of what else she'd need for this trip: water, binoculars, antidepressants, a pocket knife. Maybe some playing cards to pass the time between her and Gael. They hadn't hung out in years—who knew if they'd be able to sustain a conversation? She wished she had more stories to share with him—ones that weren't about work and stress and Grandma Jolene's declining health. But that was her life.

"Grandma?" Maya called out. "I'm leaving in a few minutes. Going on that trip, remember? I'll let you know if I see any of your favorite birds."

Maya had moved back into her grandmother's house a few years ago to care for her. Sometimes she came home from a twelve-hour workday to find Jolene had peed herself. No matter how often Maya asked her brother to help with the care, he found some excuse to avoid doing so. This time around, she offered him a hundred bucks a day to do it while she was gone, and he'd agreed within seconds—no surprise there.

"Do you remember when you took me to Gold Lake when I was little?" Maya said to Jolene. "You saw your first male wood duck and screamed, so I turned and ran, and you called after me, 'No, Maya, that was a good scream! Just look at that gorgeous duck!'"

Jolene didn't respond, but that was normal. She spent so much of her time staring out the window into the backyard. Sometimes she watched the robins and blue jays, but other times her gaze fixed on nothing in particular. She didn't seem out of it though—rather, expectant. Waiting for something to appear in some shadowy, overgrown corner of the yard. Maya worried about her grandmother getting bored, but at least she wasn't watching Fox News all day.

When Maya approached, the old woman was sitting in her recliner, still fixed on the outside world. Maya planted a kiss on her cheek and squeezed her hand.

"I'll only be gone a few days, okay?" she said. "Brandon's coming by to take care of you. If he doesn't show up, call me. I ... well, I hope I'll have cell service out there."

Expressionless, Jolene tilted her head slightly to acknowledge her granddaughter, then turned back to the window. That was that.

Her phone buzzed. It was Gael: *c u in 2 minutes*

She replied: *you texting while driving?? ;)*

Shoving a few final things in her backpack, Maya hoped she hadn't forgotten anything truly essential. It had been a while since she'd last roughed it in the wilderness, so the preparations that had once been second nature now took more deliberate thought and effort. Ironically, ever since starting her job, she'd had less and less time for enjoying the solitude of a forest or the cool calm of a lake. Mostly, she stared at a computer all day, then drove straight home from work around dark.

"Bye, Grandma!" she called out as she opened the front door.

Jolene let out a brief hum but otherwise said nothing, preoccupied with the backyard.

As soon as Maya locked the door, anxiety bubbled up inside her. What if Brandon didn't show up? She'd better message him one more time.

Don't let Grandma die, k?

Brandon replied a few seconds later with a thumbs up emoji. Not the most reassuring response, but better than nothing.

Now Maya could focus on this vacation. Time for herself, for friendship, for the beauty of nature. The thought made her tear up. She hadn't realized how much she needed this, and here it finally was.

Right then, Gael pulled up to the house in a blue Prius—a big step up from the old beater sedan Maya remembered. Hefting her heavy backpack onto her shoulders, Maya walked toward the car. Gael met her halfway down the sidewalk, grinning. Maya softened at the realization that her friend—could she still call him that?—carried that same infectious warmth as before. The world hadn't yet snuffed out his light.

"Holy shit, Maya," Gael said. He attempted to hug her, but the backpack made it difficult.

"Here, let me—"

Maya tried to slouch the backpack off, but the straps were too tight. The failed attempt made her laugh, and Gael joined in. In lieu of a hug, she grabbed his hands and squeezed.

"It's good to see you," she said. "I've missed you so much."

"Same."

An awkward pause filled the space between them, then Gael's grin lit up once more.

"You ready to see some fucking birds?" he asked.

"Oh, you bet I am."

———

Somewhere, in the hollowed-out trunk of an elm tree as old as this country, a clutch of spectral eggs twitched, cracked, and finally hatched. Downy spirits emerged, fragile as wisps, and cried out for flesh.

Chapter 2

Gael didn't mind driving the whole six hours. Taking on additional responsibility was something he'd always done—part of his older brother programming—but he sometimes wished he could be prince for a day, well cared for and freed of all his duties.

Maya sat beside him as they sped down the two-lane highway, empty save for the occasional farm truck. A field of rust-headed sorghum lay on one side, and an algae-choked lake lay on the other. It would be a few more hours before they reached the old-growth forest, but this area had once been exactly that. Centuries of conquest and development had stripped this place bare and rendered it comparatively lifeless.

"Mind if I grab the aux?" Maya asked, not waiting for a response before grabbing it.

"So long as I have veto power," Gael said, smiling. "No butt rock, obviously."

"I still don't know what that term means."

"You'll know it when you hear it. You make a road trip playlist?"

Maya flashed Gael her phone screen and a Spotify playlist titled *The Songs That Mutated My DNA Permanently*.

"It's got Gaga, it's got Rihanna, it's—"

"Oh, you better press play in the next five seconds, I swear to God," Gael said.

Bonding with Maya just like old times comforted him. Even so, memories alone couldn't sustain and grow a friendship. Maybe at some point during this trip, he'd get to know who Maya was now, years after their last real hangout.

They belted a few 2010s classics together until Gael went too hard and launched into a coughing fit. Maya burst out laughing and turned down the music.

"Water," Gael choked out. "Please."

Maya handed him a bottle, and he gulped down half of it.

"Ooh, thank you," he said. "Two weeks into the summer and I've already lost my teacher voice."

"Oh, you sing to your students, do you?" Maya said, smiling. "Replace the words in some Chappell Roan song with elements from the period table?"

Gael laughed, then went silent, his throat tightening. He hadn't told Maya about his job woes yet. Maybe now was the time.

"I, uh, well ... I'm not teaching anymore," he said. "They didn't renew my contract."

"What the fuck?" Maya said, grabbing Gael's shoulder. "Really?"

"Yeah, it's ..." Gael's eyes stung. This was the first time he'd explained it out loud to someone. He hadn't even shared the news with his sister yet. Trying to stave off tears, he continued. "One of my students found out I'm trans. Or, I guess he suspected as much and then decided to do some digging. Somehow, he found a pre-transition profile pic of me. Who the fuck knows where he got it; I really thought I'd scrubbed everything from that era. Anyway, he showed it to his mom."

"Wait, like, specifically to get you fired?"

"Maybe? This is the same kid whose mom made him sit out of our evolution unit."

"Well, fuck that kid and fuck that mom. I don't get it though. How'd you actually lose the job?"

"Well, this bitch," Gael said, gripping the steering wheel extra hard, "was part of Moms Against Gender Ideology."

"Oh, those fucking morons. Someone tell them to get real hobbies. Jesus Christ."

"Right? So, she riled up the local chapter and, together, they attended a full month of school board meetings just to complain about me. They called me a pedophile and a groomer and a confused, deranged woman. It was horrible. I was throwing up every day."

"Fucking hateful wastes of space. Some people just need to be shot," Maya said. "Or, I guess, sued for defamation. I don't know."

"I thought about suing them, but everything happened so quickly. Not long after the board meetings, my principal called me in and said they weren't renewing my contract. He didn't say it was because I'm trans, of course; he was too spineless to tell the truth. All he said was that I didn't seem like the right fit for the school, so ... buh-bye."

"Oh, Gael." Maya put her hand on his arm and rubbed it in circles. "This world is so fucking stupid and cruel. What are you going to do? Is there anything you need?"

Gael sniffled, wiped his nose. "Well, I've been looking for jobs, submitting apps to literally any place that's open. Even retail, which I promised I'd never go back to."

"Not after Claire's," Maya said.

"Oh god, don't speak her name!" Gael laughed. "Anyway, yeah, I've been too scared to apply for another education job, and I've never really had a plan B if I'm being honest. Maybe I'll find one in the woods."

Maya offered a sad smile. "Maybe the birds will have some ideas."

"Please, god, yes, let's talk about birds. Anything other than my old job."

"Ooh, okay," Maya said. "Um, which bird do you want to see the most on this trip?"

"A cerulean warbler," Gael said almost instantly. This was one of the things he loved most about birding—how infectiously energizing it could be.

"That'd be incredible," Maya said. "But I'm going for something even cooler: a whip-poor-will. You know how long I've wanted to—?"

"Of course, I do," Gael said. "You mention the same bird every trip! I'll be getting a good night's sleep while you're up squinting into the dark."

"Well, okay, what about something even *rarer*? What about..." Maya grinned and paused, as if uncertain how to finish her joke.

Gael got to the punchline before her. "Oh, I know," he said. "An ivory-billed woodpecker. Back from extinction and right in front of our faces. I'd shit myself."

"Hard same," Maya said. "Good thing I brought an extra pair of underwear."

They laughed together, and Gael knew this trip would be one to cherish.

———◦———

Despite Maya's best efforts to stay awake and help with navigation, the vibration of the country road soothed her into sleep. She dreamt of Grandma Jolene staring out the window and talking to some unseen entity. "It's so good to see you again," she said. "How long has it been? Sixty years? Sixty thousand? I'd invite you in for coffee, but I don't think you—"

A frantic tap on the knee cut Maya's dream short. She opened her eyes, feeling momentarily stuck between dimensions. Naps always did this to her; it was why she never took them if she could help it.

"What is it?" she asked. The car wasn't moving. "Shit, I can give you directions if—"

Gael still had his hand on her knee, but he was looking out the front window, keeping his head low. Had he spotted a bucket list bird on the road? That would explain why they were parked on the shoulder.

"Look," he said, pointing covertly.

A string of logging vehicles pulled onto the country road, loaded with stacks of ancient wood, severed trunks ringed hundreds of times over. The funeral procession drove past Gael's Prius in clouds of dust and exhaust, rumbling forth an industrial dirge.

"Goddamnit," Gael said, punching his steering wheel. "I didn't fucking realize it would..."

As soon the dust cleared, Maya saw it. This part of the forest—or what used to be a forest—had been clear cut. Stumps littered the ground like tombstones, and massive tire treads scarred the bare dirt in chaotic zig-zags. She had to squint to see where the surviving forest continued, up a long slope far in the distance.

"You couldn't have known, Gael," Maya said, squeezing his am. "The map probably wasn't updated, and who knows how quickly they've been clearing this place. Maybe it *was* a forest when you made the plan."

"I don't even want to think about that," Gael said. He pinched his eyes shut with his thumb and forefinger.

Maya was coming out of her haze and desperate to help.

"Yeah, it's fucked," she said. "But—well, I mean, we can change the plan. Look at that area way up ahead. Still has trees, right? Probably still has birds, too. I know you had some good trails mapped out—"

"So many good trails!" Gael interrupted, smacking the dashboard with each syllable.

"—but we can still make it work. No need to call the whole thing off. Let's spend time together! Let's see some fucking birds!"

"And what about the loggers?" Gael asked. "That corporation probably owns the land. They'll kick us out or worse if they catch us."

"So we'll try not to be caught," Maya said. "Ask for forgiveness, not permission, right? And hell, we used to trespass a ton in Earth Unity Alliance. Remember those cops who chased us outside that fur farm?"

"My blood pressure sure remembers," Gael said. "I don't know. I'm more nervous about stuff like that these days, and I'm also a brown dude, Maya. Shit's riskier for me."

Maya couldn't argue with that, but she didn't want to give up her chance to reconnect with both nature and an old friend.

"Listen, I'll be my sweetest white lady self if we get caught," she said. "I'll be like, *oh, sir, I'm so, so sorry for trespassing! We just saw the prettiest flowers in the forest and wanted to pick them. Would you like a honeysuckle?*"

Gael snorted and shook his head. "Okay, but don't ask them if they want a honeysuckle. They might get the wrong idea."

Maya gave Gael a playful smack on the arm.

"So we'll do it?" she asked.

"Yeah, we'll do it," Gael replied. "And shit, if we get imprisoned for trespassing, at least I'll have a place to stay and something to eat when my savings runs out."

Maya wasn't sure if she should laugh. Maybe jokes were Gael's only way to cope.

"Well, there we go," Maya said. "Let's find somewhere to park."

Gael put the car into drive, pulled off the shoulder of the road, and sped ahead. "Hopefully, we'll get there before the loggers do."

———————

Gael squinted into the treeline, gold light illuminating what remained of the forest. The trees were host to abundant but diminishing life, soft mosses and tangled ivy blanketing the sweeps of burled trunks. Silhouetted in shadow, the occasional bird darted from branch to branch. Not bucket list birds, but chittering little house wrens. Gael didn't hold that against them though. Even if they were common, they were cute.

"That's a good spot," Maya said. She pointed to an area off the road choked with towers of elderberry shrubs, white flowers in full bloom.

Gael eased the car into the gentle ditch. Gravel skittered and nettles crunched under the tires. From this side of the elderberries, the road was hardly visible. Gael parked and let out a sigh.

"Well, hope this works," he said.

"I'm sure it will," Maya said.

Opening the door, Gael eyed a patch of poison oak below. He was glad to be wearing jeans. Sure, it'd get hot, but at least he wouldn't leave this place with a nasty rash.

"Shit," Maya said, looking up from her unzipped backpack. "I knew I'd forgotten something. You got any bug spray?"

"Oh, sorry, I'm here for the ticks, not the birds, so I don't believe in bug spray," Gael said.

Maya rolled her eyes and gestured for Gael to hand it over. He grabbed a bottle of bug spray from his backpack's side pocket and tossed it over the car. Maya caught it and got to work, spraying herself liberally.

"God, I'm remembering this student I had who was obsessed with living in a tent in the woods someday," Gael said. "He did this final project about it for my Biology class. Researched the plants he could eat, the process for collecting and purifying water, all that. And by the time he researched tick-borne illnesses, he was like, 'nope, never mind. I'll stay in the city.' Loved that kid."

"Wish I could've seen you teach," Maya said, tossing the bug spray back over. "I bet you were great with those kids. Thanks, by the way."

"No problem." A hollow ache filled Gael's gut. Not hunger, but a deeper yearning for the world he'd been cut away from like a scrap of fat.

"Don't take this the wrong way, but you were lucky with that job," Maya said, squirting some sunscreen into her hands. "Some people never find a job they love. I thought I'd love mine, but most days I wake up hoping someone will T-bone me on my way to the office."

"Well, I certainly don't feel lucky," he said, a bitter edge creeping into his tone. "And at least you have a job."

Maya stopped applying her sunscreen and looked at Gael. "Okay, fair. My bad."

Even when they were younger, Gael never found Maya's apologies satisfying. Not that he wanted them to be long and self-flagellating, but their brevity left much to be desired. Some things about her would never change.

"Why do you hate your job so much anyway?" Gael asked. "I'll be honest. I don't even really know what you do."

"Oh, I'm an 'avian advocate' at Songbird Stewards," Maya said, using finger quotes. "I wish I could say I did something useful there, but I don't think that's ever been true. Like, the nonprofit works completely within this system that's destroying our fucking world while receiving funds from the people who benefit most from that destruction. The incentive to create actual change just isn't there. It's meaningless, symbolic work more than anything, but here I am, grinding my bones to dust for the job. Us breaking chickens out of farms with Earth Unity Alliance felt way more useful."

"Still can't believe we never got arrested. That version of me feels like a totally different person," Gael said. "Anyway, fuck talking about work. It's the only thing some of my teacher friends ever talk about, and it's exhausting. Like, don't you have a life outside of what you do for money?"

Maya laughed. "I mean, for some people, no. I'm fucking exhausted by the time I get home. I have enough energy to change Grandma's diaper, feed her, and then fall asleep halfway through a TV show. It's sad."

"Well, if Jolene is looking to hire a new diaper changer, I'm on the job market again."

They both burst into laughter, and tension from the moment prior eased. Gael smiled at his friend.

"Alright, let's go find that ivory-billed woodpecker," he said, locking up the car.

"In your fucking dreams," Maya said.

Together, they hiked into the woods.

Chapter 3

The friends stayed silent for the first few minutes of their hike, a habit carried over from birding trips of the past. After all, the more they talked, the less likely they were to hear birds and the less likely birds were to stick around.

Late afternoon was hardly prime birding time, but even so, Maya had expected more lively chirping and chattering. Shrunken as it was, what remained of this forest was still ancient, home to abundant life for thousands of years. Why so quiet all of a sudden?

Treading with a lighter step, Maya listened closer. From somewhere in the canopy came the feeble buzz of a cicada. Then, farther ahead, the clatter of a squirrel in chase. In the distance beyond, a cardinal's persistent *pew pew pew pew*.

Maya picked up on something else, too. The sound—if it was a sound—didn't come from a specific direction, but rather, everywhere and nowhere. Something buried just under the hot, dry wind blowing through the forest. She stopped in place.

"Need a sec to rest?" Gael asked, wiping sweat from his forehead. "Or see something interesting?"

Maya didn't answer, instead looking at her friend and assessing his expression. Did he pick up on it, too? Some ubiquitous, unplaceable murmur at the edge of perception. Voices? Animal noises? Or just wind whistling through leaves dry as tinder and howling through the hollows of long-dead trees?

"Don't you hear it?" she asked.

Gael cocked his head and waited. After a moment, he smiled. "I need to stop listening to music so loud on my runs."

"It's—" Maya struggled for the right words. The mystery of the sound—hallucination?—gnawed at her, and she knew it would keep doing so until she found her answer. "Shit, I don't know what it is."

"Well, that's okay," Gael said. "Let's rest for a bit. Ooh!"

Before Maya could ask what he was reacting to, Gael reached into a bush loaded with fruit—green, translucent, and veiny. Not appetizing to look at, but he popped one in his mouth and chewed.

"Gooseberries," he said, handing one to Maya.

"Are they good?" she asked.

Gael shrugged, then laughed with his mouth full. "Not really, but it's something to eat if we get lost."

Maya grinned. "You better not be poisoning me," she said, then sampled one. The fruit was sour and slightly dry, like it hadn't soaked up enough rain. Still, she swallowed it. "I think I'll stick to my protein bars."

"Same," Gael said.

Their conversation fell into silence, and that underlying sound or sensation crept in once more. Something about it made Maya ache in ways she could hardly describe. A yearning for something lost. Or a lost thing yearning to be found again, to be nurtured. It made Maya feel powerless. She wanted something—anything—to distract her.

And then it came: a loud wooden drilling sound.

"Goddamnit," Gael said, crouching low. "Is that the loggers?"

"Shh," Maya said, holding up a hand. When the sound returned, she smiled. "That's a big-ass woodpecker. It's got to be a pileated. I've only ever seen one."

Gael shook his head and put on an embarrassed half-smile. "Sorry. Paranoia brain."

"You take an edible or something?"

"You know, I totally forgot to bring them. You still an indica girlie? I should've—"

The drilling cut Gael short. It came from somewhere nearby, but the sound warped around the trees almost like a Doppler effect pitch shift.

"Weird," Maya said. Despite the heat, her skin prickled.

"Yeah," Gael replied. "Want to find this thing?"

Maya nodded. Together, they crept forward. Maya walked with a light step, careful not to snap any twigs. Again, the drilling echoed out somewhere up ahead. Maya's heart thumped in her chest. Tangled with the adrenaline of the hunt was an underlying dread, but she didn't let the feeling stop her.

A few feet ahead, the deer trail narrowed, choked between two massive white oaks, hundreds of years old. As soon as Maya stepped between these guardians of the forest, something clicked. It wasn't the natural click of an insect, but rather, something artificial. Frozen in place, she looked for its source.

"Shit," she said, not as quiet as she'd been a mere minute ago.

"What?" Gael asked, shrinking into a crouch once more.

"A trail cam." Another click. Definitely the camera. "I think it belongs to that logging company. There's a sticker here with the same name I saw on those vehicles."

Maya tried to imagine why the logging company needed a trailcam. No chance they cared about monitoring local wildlife—just trespassers interfering with their operation. Now they had Maya's face—maybe Gael's, too. There was no telling how many other trail cams the friends had passed without realizing. Some security person—or maybe even the cops—could already be on their way. But even if that were the case, she could charm them in her best innocent white woman voice.

"Fuck it," Maya said. She pulled a melted chocolate protein bar out of her backpack and smeared it across the trail cam's lens. "Now we have some privacy."

"Maya, holy shit," Gael said, sweat beading on his forehead.

"We'll be okay," she said. "Just, I don't know, keep an eye out for other cameras."

The woodpecker's drilling echoed through the forest again.

Gael narrowed his eyes, and the slighted grin crept onto his face. "We gotta find that fucking bird."

———————

The woodpecker went quiet before they could find it, but at least they'd set up camp nearby. The area wasn't so much a clearing as it was a space between trees just large enough for a two-person tent. They had to flatten a bed of nettles and clear some rocky dirt clods, but once the tent was up, it felt cozy enough.

Gael hadn't realized how tiring the drive and hike had been until he laid on his sleeping bag. Almost immediately, his eyes fluttered, shutting for seconds at a time before opening again. In this state of too-warm half-consciousness, he watched Maya through the open flap while she scanned the canopy with her binoculars.

She called out birds as she saw them. A brown thrasher one minute and a yellow-billed cuckoo a few minutes later. Each bird was beautiful in its own right, but not enough to get Gael off his back and out of the tent. Maya's descriptions of the birds brought him peace and comfort.

"It's plucking its plumage," she said. "A white feather is floating to the ground."

"Grab it for me?" Gael said, half-joking.

"Oh, so I'm supposed to do everything around here?" Maybe her response was intended to be silly, but her words seemed distant, distracted. Gael sensed Maya's mind had been elsewhere ever since they entered the forest, and he couldn't figure out why. Was she thinking about work? Feeling the awkwardness of their reunion? More worried about cops and logging company security than she let on? He'd ask her about it later tonight.

Shadows grew long as the evening approached, but the birds didn't burst into their expected dinnertime chatter. A solemn silence took hold, broken only by the occasional chirping cricket or gust of humid wind. The forest should have been brimming with noisy life, but maybe the birds sensed this place wasn't long for this world. Maybe most of them had moved on or died.

Then came the drilling from a tree behind the tent—still sounding slightly unnatural, warping before it reached Gael's ears. Maya was so quick to whip around that she nearly lost her footing.

"It's back," she whisper-shouted. "Get up."

Gael peeled his sweaty body off the sleeping bag and felt around the cramped tent for his binoculars. As soon as he found them, he joined his friend.

Maya white-knuckled her binoculars. "Oh my God," she said. "It really is a pileated. About two-thirds the way up, near that dead branch."

Gael struggled to locate the bird and feared it would fly off. But soon, his gaze landed on it. And really, how could he miss it?

The woodpecker was huge—far bigger than the red-bellied or red-headed woodpeckers Gael sometimes saw in town. High up in an elm tree, the bird poked its head into a large hole. The prospect that it might have a nest filled Gael with joy. But something wasn't right about the bird. Something he couldn't yet pinpoint.

"This is so fucking cool," Maya said. "I honestly didn't think I'd ever see one."

"No," Gael said. His voice quivered as a realization hatched inside him. "That's not a pileated."

"Oh, come on. What else would it be?" Maya said. "We don't get any other woodpeckers this big—"

"Wait until it pulls out of the hole again. Look at its bill. Look at its markings." Gael sounded deadly serious, like he was on the verge of breaking.

"Maybe a female?" Maya asked, squinting through her binoculars as the woodpecker's head twitched. "Their cheeks look different, right?" But even as those words came out of her mouth, Gael sensed she was reaching the same realization. A truth that seemed impossible.

"It's an ivory-billed woodpecker," Gael said, pulling his binoculars away and steadying himself against a tree.

"I—no. How?"

"Look at the fucking markings," Gael replied. "They match."

The woodpecker's crest was mostly bright red with a strip of black up front. Its bill was cream-colored instead of the pileated's charcoal, and the bottoms of its wings were white instead of black.

"Holy shit," Maya said.

Gael felt lightheaded and tight in his throat, like he might pass out at any second. A plume of heat rose from the forest floor, and as soon as it greeted him, he stumbled back and fell on his ass. At the *thump*, the woodpecker flew off deeper into the woods, its wingbeats loud.

Maya didn't yell at Gael though. She seemed stunned in her own way, as if she'd been turned to stone. A few seconds passed before she plopped down beside him, apparently without regard for the stinging nettles.

"I really thought they were gone for good," Gael said. "Like, we were just talking about them. How did we get so lucky?"

"And that looks like a nest, doesn't it?" Maya replied, her words coming out thin and choked. She was crying.

Gael was crying now, too, joy and wonder spilling out of him. But when he looked at Maya, a darkness clouded her expression. Gael had seen this look from his students during class discussions about climate change. A look of despair for the future, of powerlessness in a dying world. Earth's lifeblood was boiling, and here his students were, sleep deprived, stuck in a poorly air-conditioned school, and bound to a bell schedule.

How soon would the logging company annihilate this part of the forest—and the ivory-billed woodpecker with it? If that trail cam was any indication, the loggers had big plans for the area.

"We need to do something," Maya said.

She was right. But Gael struggled to imagine how they could prevent what felt inevitable. He thought back to those climate change conversations with his students, how he'd mustered all his energy to rouse them to action and instill a sense of cautious optimism. It had felt like the right thing at the time, but even then, he'd barely believed the words coming out of his mouth. To feel so consumed with despair and still preach hope—did that make him a fraud? No. He didn't think so. In fact, he suspected there were many others like him who privately carried that hopelessness and acted anyway, even if they felt their actions would accomplish little to nothing. What other way was there to live?

———◦———

"You still in touch with any Earth Unity Alliance people?" Gael asked. "They might be able to help."

"Shh, I'm filming," Maya said, pointing her phone at the ivory-billed woodpecker perched outside its nest.

Or was it a nest? Each time the bird left as if to get food for its young, it returned empty-beaked. Its movements were sudden, almost manic, as if it needed something it couldn't find or express.

When it flew off again, Maya stopped filming and turned to Gael. "You're right," she said. "I think Morgan and Brian are still doing stuff with them. Well, maybe not Brian. I haven't seen him post in a while. Maybe he went off the grid like he was always talking about."

That last comment came out more snide than she'd intended, and immediately she felt bad. So what if Brian had gone off the grid? At least he was saying he'd do something and following through. Living in alignment with his beliefs. Maya couldn't always say the same for herself.

"Okay," Gael said. "So, what if we post about the bird? Do a livestream call to action or something. I mean, we get cell service out here, which somehow feels wrong, but I guess everywhere is close to civilization these days."

"I think that plan's just about as good as any," Maya said, readying her phone for the woodpecker's return. They waited a minute, and when it didn't appear, she continued the conversation. "You ever think about rejoining the group? I sometimes miss it."

"I didn't feel like I could," Gael said. "It's embarrassing, but I was afraid that if I got arrested, I'd get fired from my teaching job. Shit, if I'd known the firing part would happen anyway, maybe I would have. Or maybe not. God, I was always so busy all the time. Too much shit to grade."

"Yeah, I feel you there," Maya said. "I thought about going back a lot, but I always had some excuse or another. I don't know. Maybe I'm lazy. Or a coward. A sellout."

"Why not all three?"

Maya laughed a humorless laugh and smacked Gael on the shoulder. Gael gave her a light tap, and it took Maya a moment to realize he was silently directing her attention back to the tree. The woodpecker had returned.

Pulling up Facebook and starting a live video, she zoomed in on the bird and began softly narrating. The image wasn't great—strangely hazy around the bird's feathered edges—but it was good enough to distinguish the distinct features of the ivory-billed woodpecker. Maya only hoped the Earth Unity Alliance folks would see the video and believe her.

"Okay, I need you to trust me when I say that we are witnessing a live ivory-billed woodpecker," she said as she filmed. "We're going to have a lot of people in the comments saying this is a pileated or a hoax or just a potato-quality video, but trust me, I'm not desperate enough to post something like this for attention or money. What I *do* want is your help—ah, see? It's hopping along the tree. And that hole right beside it, Gael and I think that's its nest. Anyway—we need your help. This forest—shit, I don't remember what the area is called. I'll drop a pin in the comments so you can find it. Anyway, this forest is being clear cut, and this woodpecker—maybe the last of its kind—could lose its territory very, very soon. I'm calling on anyone who even remotely gives a shit about the natural world—bird lovers, tree huggers, future life on Earth value-ers—to help us stop this logging operation. Join us. We'll be waiting."

With that, Maya ended the livestream and quickly posted the location data in the comments. Views, likes, and comments were already pouring in.

"Damn, you rehearse that or what?" Gael asked.

"Nah, I give a lot of presentations at work," Maya responded. "Normally with fewer curse words."

Right as she was about to put her phone away, a text popped up on her screen. Brandon with an update: *jsyk, grandma's still alive. Still looking out the window as always, lol. When you gonna pay me btw?*

In her excitement about the woodpecker, Maya had forgotten all about her grandmother and, mercifully, her brother too. She didn't bother responding to the text, but instead Venmoed him half of what she'd promised. He could have the rest when she got back if he did a good job.

Maya put away her phone and observed the bird with Gael. She sensed the woodpecker was observing them back. It was probably just protecting its nest from potential threats, but Maya couldn't shake the feeling that it wanted something from them. Something more than rallying the environmentalist troops.

She closed her eyes and tried tuning in to the sounds of the forest she'd heard before—the sounds below the sounds. As crazy as it seemed, she had a gut feeling she'd find a message in those spectral murmurs. A directive from the woodpecker itself.

A twig snapped behind Maya and Gael. The bird flew off, and the friends spun to see what was behind them.

An old, long-bearded man stood there, shotgun slung across his shoulder, logging company logo adorning his sweaty base-ball cap. Either his approach had been stealthy or Maya and Gael had been too entranced to notice.

"This is private property," the man said, clutching his gun in both hands. He glanced at Maya briefly, then squinted at Gael for a long moment. "Pack your shit."

Maya felt flustered but knew this was her time to put on the harmless white lady act. Maybe she could convince the old man to look the other way.

"I'm so sorry, sir!" she said. "We didn't realize. We just thought it was a beautiful forest and wanted to see some wildlife."

She gestured toward the woodpecker only to realize it had flown off again. She wondered if it would be worth mentioning what the logging company would be doing by destroying the bird's habitat, but the man probably wouldn't give a shit.

The man tightened his grip on the gun, and his sunburnt face grew redder. "I saw you on camera, smearing your shit all over the lens."

It was chocolate, Maya thought but didn't say. She struggled for a response.

"Listen, sir," Gael said, taking a step forward.

The old man straightened his posture and puffed out his chest, as if preparing for an attack.

"I—I'm not going to do anything," Gael said. "I'm just asking if we can stay one night. Our tent is already up, and it's getting dark. I promise we'll—"

"Enough," the man said, cocking the shotgun. "No need for cops. I can handle you both myself."

Maya wasn't sure why she started laughing—the stress of the moment or the man's over-the-top reaction—but once it began, she had no way of stopping it. Gael looked at her, wide-eyed and speechless, his expression begging her to shut up, to stop endangering them. Even then, she felt powerless to do anything.

The old man lurched toward Maya, close enough that she could smell his beef jerky breath. "Nothing about this is funny, bitch."

"For real, we're not looking for trouble," Gael said, holding out his hands as if he were keeping a rabid dog at bay. "Please, we'll—"

"You'll what?" the man asked, shifting his attention to Gael and pointing the gun directly at his chest.

Maya stopped laughing at once, her body frozen. She wanted to react but had never been in a situation like this before.

The man took a step toward Gael, then another, and another.

"Sir, stop," Gael said in a thin whisper, as if he were afraid speaking too loud would startle the man into shooting. "Stay right there."

The man grinned, taking one last step forward, and dug the shotgun's muzzle into Gael's chest. When at last he spoke, his voice exuded a sadist's satisfaction. "And what are you gonna do if I—"

Before the man could finish his sentence, Gael shoulder-checked him.

Maya witnessed it happen in slow motion: the gun flying from his hands and skittering into the shadowy underbrush; the man tumbling backward, arms windmilling but failing to stabilize; his head striking the thick, unearthed root of an ancient tree; the crack of bone instead of bullet. Silence that stretched on too long.

"Oh no," Gael said, kneeling beside the old man and squeezing his hand. "Sir, are you okay? I didn't mean to—I just, well, I panicked and..."

Maya crouched at the old man's other side, then gently tilted his head. Shattered vertebrae crunched with the slight movement. Blood, thick and sticky, strung from the man's skull to the tree's root.

Noticing the injury, Gael cursed and jumped into chest compressions, letting out a "shit" with each repetition. After several pumps, he pinched the old man's nose shut and delivered two breaths.

Maya watched, realizing before Gael that CPR would do no good. She waited through one more round of compressions and breaths before grabbing Gael's hands and shaking her head.

"No," he said, his eyes wet with tears. "I was just trying to—I didn't mean to..."

His words dissolved into sobs, and Maya pulled him into a hug. Gael buried his face into her chest and heaved. Maya's heart was pounding.

"It's okay," she said, wishing she hadn't frozen up. How might this moment have played out differently if she'd stepped in? Used what privilege she had to protect them both? Maybe it would've done nothing, her femininity and whiteness no match for the man's aggression. "You were only trying to keep us safe."

While Gael sobbed, Maya watched blood ooze from the old man's fractured neck and skull. It dripped like honey into the parched dirt of the forest floor.

She scanned the area for other trail cams. Anything that might have recorded the moment. The first one had caught her vandalizing logging company property, but maybe Gael's manslaughter had escaped notice. She saw no signs that they were being watched, but that did little to ease her mind.

What the hell would they do now?

Before she could answer that question, Gael looked up at her, his face a mess of tear-streaked dirt.

"You won't turn me in, will you?" he asked.

"Jesus fucking Christ, of course not. Who do you think I am?" Maya said. It didn't matter that she'd barely spoken to Gael these past several years. Some loyalties never changed. And in any case, she had to atone for her inaction.

Gael closed his eyes and took a deep breath. After a long pause, he spoke again: "Then will you help me with the body?"

———————

Thank God there was a cliff near their campsite. Gael wasn't sure he could get away with the old man's death, but he stood a better chance if it looked more like a tragic fall—which it was. *It was an accident, it was an accident, it was an accident...* He let the thought cycle as if through repetition he might come to believe it. *If I hadn't pushed him, he wouldn't have—NO. It was an accident.*

"Gael."

Maya's voice snapped him back to reality. She hunched over the body, holding the man's limp legs. Piss had soaked through his jeans, and a fecal stench hung in the humid air. Gael remembered teaching his Biology students what happened after people died—how the dead often released their bladders and bowels.

He'd had the attention of every single one of his students that day, and he'd taken note: lessons about death and shit are great for engagement.

"My bad, I spaced out," Gael said. He grabbed the man's calloused, cooling hands once more. They slipped slightly in Gael's sweaty grip, and he imagined the skin degloving—the process of decay and disintegration beginning impossibly fast.

"I'm sorry," Maya said.

"For what?" Gael asked, but even in his dazed state, he knew. He just wanted to hear Maya say it out loud.

"I should have done more," she said. "Like, done *anything at all* when he came after you. I was a coward."

"Thanks." He let the moment hang for a few seconds, feeling the weight of the man in his forearms. "I really don't know if I would've done anything different in your shoes. I'm a coward sometimes, too."

He thought back to the school board meeting he'd attended to defend himself and the bigoted mom who'd screamed him into submission. The way his body shrank before her red-faced vitriol. He hated that part of himself.

"I don't know how much you stepping in would've changed anything. No use dwelling on it," Gael said. "Anyway, let's just take care of this body."

A flutter overhead caught his attention. There it perched: the ivory-billed woodpecker, its mohawked silhouette unmistakable in the dark orange glow of dusk. He couldn't see the bird's eyes, but he knew it was looking down at them.

"I don't think I've ever had a more eventful hour in my fucking life," Gael said.

"Yeah," Maya said, staring back at the bird. "Craziest roller coaster I've ever been on."

Gael let out a humorless laugh. "And it's making me sick."

"Same."

Still holding the old man's corpse with the shotgun slung around his shoulder, the friends shimmied to the edge of the cliff. The drop was probably fifty feet, enough to kill a person, and ended in a mostly dry creek bed with the tiniest vein of water trickling through its center. Gael wondered when this creek was last full to brimming. He pictured deer and raccoons and mountain lions lapping from its abundance, catfish and gar floating lazily in its cool currents. Those days—if they'd ever existed—were long gone.

"Ready?" Maya asked. "On three."

Gael took a deep breath, then nodded.

"One ..." They swung the old man and his gun toward the ledge. "Two ..." With greater momentum. "Three!" And flung him to his resting place.

Gael flinched when the body hit the ground, but there was no splatter or crack. Only a dull thud. A puff of dust rose around the old man, particles floating skyward like a soul departing.

When the cloud cleared, a pit formed in Gael's gut: the man had landed facedown. Even from this height, he could see the bloody injury on the back of his head and neck. If someone with the slightest intelligence stumbled upon the scene, they'd know something was fishy.

"We need to go down and flip him," Gael said. "It has to look natural."

Maya closed her eyes and paused for a long moment. "Can we do it in the morning? It's late. No one else is going to see him tonight, and it's dangerous trying to climb down a cliff when it's this dark."

Gael knew she was right, but he hated feeling like there was even the slightest chance of discovery. He thought about what life in prison would be like for him. What if they denied him his hormones and forcibly detransitioned him? He'd heard of it happening to trans people before, and the thought made him quake with fury. The life he'd fought so hard for, siphoned away in a cell.

"Okay," he said. "But first thing in the morning—literally first thing—I'm going down there. I don't want Earth Unity Alliance people to come here based on your video and find him."

"The cliff is far enough away from the nest," Maya said. "We can keep people distracted if they do come."

Another flutter from above: the woodpecker. The last bits of daylight caught its eyes, and Gael realized what the bird was staring at: the old man's corpse.

"It's been following us," Maya said. She smiled as if she couldn't help but feel delighted despite the circumstances.

"It sure has," Gael said, more muted than his friend but still feeling that faint spark of excitement and disbelief. "Let's go to sleep, if we even can."

Chapter 4

It took Maya hours to fall asleep but barely a second to lurch back into consciousness. A sound pulled her out of one night-mare and into another. Whatever it was, it didn't fit with the forest's other nocturnal noises: buzzing mosquitos and sum-mer-scorched leaves rustling in a dry wind. No, this was an artificial sound.

As Maya's bleariness cleared, she realized what it was: a phone ringing. Not her own, which she'd turned off, and not Gael's at the edge of the tent, but the old man's, echoing up from the bottom of the cliff. His chosen ringtone was the classic rotary phone ring, and it occurred to Maya just then how old the man was. *Like killing my dad*, she thought, then quickly pushed the idea away.

Gael snored lightly beside her, apparently undisturbed. Was he sleeping soundly, even after what had happened? A dark part of Maya hoped his dreams were just as polluted with horror as her own had been.

The phone stopped ringing. A few seconds of silence fol-lowed, and then the ringing began again.

Maya tried to picture who might be trying to reach the old man. His spouse, probably. Someone he lived with who was still up at the witching hour, praying for the man to come home safe. Eventually, they would call the cops, and then—

Enough, Maya thought. If she was going to be awake and worked up, she might as well do something with her anxious energy. She unzipped the tent and slipped hiking boots over her bare feet. Not wanting Gael to wake up with a thousand mosquito bites, she closed the tent flap before leaving.

It had been ages since she'd last immersed herself in a darkness this complete. In fact, few places this dark still existed. Above, the writhing canopy choked out the stars, and the moon didn't dare show its face. Even as her eyes adjusted, her surroundings appeared only in the darkest gray silhouettes—trees like Roman columns enclosing her on all sides.

Again, the phone rang. She considered walking to the cliff and looking down at the body, but she imagined herself tumbling over the edge by accident, the second in a growing stack of corpses. No, she'd stay right where she was and calm herself with deep breaths. The night air felt swamp like, and she yearned for the years when summer nights still got cool.

Then, a silver-blue shape caught her attention. Squinting two-thirds the way up a tree, she struggled to discern what it was. A dull bioluminescent fungus? No, it was moving. And this was the woodpecker's tree.

Fumbling in the dark, Maya navigated back to the tent, unzipping it and reaching inside for her binoculars.

"What's going on?" Gael muttered, half-asleep as he rolled over.

"Nothing, keep sleeping," Maya said.

She took a moment to relocate the glowing spot, then lifted her binoculars.

There. A tiny beak and face poked out of that hole in the elm tree. So it *was* a nest! An electric energy coursed through Maya. More than one woodpecker remained. Maybe the species stood a chance at survival after all.

But the longer she looked, the more confused she felt. Why, with no discernible light source, did the fledgling appear to be glowing? Maybe it was a trick of the eyes or a sleep-deprived brain. She'd probably be better off crawling back into the tent and passing out for a few hours.

The phone rang again. Maya lowered her binoculars, closed her eyes, and counted down, waiting for the sound to stop. Three rings ... four ... five ... silence.

But not quite silence. From the base of the elm tree came another sound—or many sounds on top of one another. They were subtle but persistent, like the static of a radio left on at the lowest volume. The most distinct manifestation of the sound or sensation Maya had first detected when entering the forest.

She approached, taking one cautious step at a time as it grew louder. Soon, her hand was on the elm tree, her ear pressed against its bark. And there she heard it.

A cacophony buried deep within the rings of the trunk, walking the line between physical and ethereal. The *clack clack clacking* of a thousand tiny beaks, hammering on their prison and begging for release.

Maya pulled away, dizzy and disoriented. All of this was too much for her brain to handle in a single day. If she went to sleep now, she might wake up and find the world normal again—no one dead, nothing changed, everything perfectly explainable. The thought comforted her; it also made her sick.

Chapter 5

The rumble and grind of logging vehicles greeted Gael as he stumbled out of the tent. The sounds were distant, but still too close for comfort, and he wondered if they'd gradually get louder throughout the day as the crew cut deeper into the heart of the woods.

Maya was already up, looking over the edge of the cliff through her binoculars. Gael's gut twisted as he remembered what she was looking at. How he'd managed to sleep was a mystery, but that was one of his body's great gifts—the ability to sleep through storms both literal and emotional.

He grabbed a gallon jug of water and walked toward his friend.

"Maya," he said.

She jumped, as if she hadn't heard his approach. Dark rings surrounded her eyes, and her face looked paler than usual.

"Water?" Gael asked, offering the jug. "I always feel better after I—"

"You need to see this." She took the jug and handed him her binoculars.

Gael tried to imagine what he'd see at the bottom of the cliff. Yellow caution tape and a whole precinct of cops surrounding the old man's body? Or maybe even no body at all? He doubted the man could've survived both falls and crawled away, but if the past 24 hours had proved anything, it was that the impossible was possible. He raised the binoculars.

No caution tape. No cops. Old man still present—still dead. But he was in worse shape than before. Bloodier and—what was that substance on him? A silvery-blue sheen clinging to his exposed guts.

"What is that shit?" Gael asked.

Before Maya could respond, the extinct woodpecker swooped into Gael's vision, landing on the corpse. It burrowed its white beak into the man's throat, then emerged a second later with a wormlike tendon. When the bird flew off, more of that silvery-blue sheen was covering the eviscerated throat. On the man's chest was another bite, much larger than the bird's—an entire pec ripped away in one go. Whatever had done this had also left the strange substance behind.

"Gael, come quick!"

The hair on Gael's neck stood on end as he lowered the binoculars and ran to his friend. The logging vehicle sounds still polluted the air, and he imagined one of the loggers stumbling upon their camp—the scene of the crime.

"Look up in the tree," Maya said. "I've already seen it, but you need to, too. Otherwise, you won't understand."

Gael followed Maya's finger to the nest. There, the woodpecker chewed the old man's tendon and prepared to regurgitate it for its young. In that instant, Gael both saw the fledglings and saw *through* them: beaks open and soundlessly begging, the tree's splintered interior visible through their translucence. One of the young beat the others to the meal and gobbled down the tendon mush. Immediately, the fledgling's body became opaque and its cries for more pierced the air.

"What the fuck," Gael said.

"I saw it last night," Maya said. "The ghostly shit, I mean. I thought I was hallucinating."

Gael felt a full-body rush at the implication. If a little meal could bring back the dead—were they dead?—then...

"I know we should get out of here before shit goes down, but I have an idea," Gael said. "Don't know if it will work, but—"

He rushed back to the tent, opened his bag of beef jerky, and dumped its contents below the woodpecker's tree. Gesturing to Maya, they both stepped away and waited.

The bird clung to the bark near its nest for a moment, cocking its head at the humans as if to assess their threat. The standoff continued for another minute while the not-too-far-off noise of buzzing saws and falling trees filled the air. Then, with little warning, the bird swooped and landed near the jerky. It poked at the offering with its beak, moving pieces around like a child playing with unwanted vegetables. Without taking any, it flew off toward the old man's corpse.

Not a minute later, the bird returned to its nest with a pinky toe. After the parent chewed it into a manageable paste, one of its ghostly fledglings devoured it in a single gulp, its body immediately gaining flesh of its own.

"I feel like I'm dreaming," Gael said.

"I kind of wish I was," Maya said. "But also ... not really."

"I know exactly what you mean."

"How long do you think it'll be before that body is gone?"

"Probably not long, but we'd need to get rid of whatever they don't eat," Gael said. "I don't plan on going to prison."

"What about this? We pack up our stuff, find a way to the bottom of the cliff, and—"

The sound of voices cut her short—several close by. They spoke in whispers that sounded both tense and excited. Another minute and they'd reach the camp.

"I really hope we're not getting fucking scammed by some AI shit here," one voice said.

"Shit, okay. Good, I guess. It's birders, not loggers," Gael said, taking a deep breath. "Um, I guess we should act normal and try to keep them away from the body. Oh, and don't mention whatever the fuck is going on with the fledglings."

"Got it," Maya replied. "Just try to play it cool for once. Remember how suspicious you used to act whenever you used your fake ID at bars?"

"Well, uh, hopefully I'm better at pretending nowadays."

Gael paced back and forth, searching for something to do that would make him look as normal as possible. When Maya sat on a fallen log, he joined her. He was tempted to strike up a fake conversation, but overselling it would work against them.

Soon, the group appeared around the bend, their leader a gorgeous butch woman with a slicked-back mohawk, staring intently at her phone.

"It should be here," she said, scrutinizing what must have been either a map or the image Maya had posted.

Gael wondered if he should wave—it was normal to wave, right?—but realized right then that he knew the woman: Morgan. They'd dated a few years back when Gael was still in Earth Unity Alliance. Nothing serious—just a few fun months. They'd even gone birding together once, the rare hangout outside of the group's regular meetings and actions. Gael remembered them sneaking off the trail to make out. They hadn't seen many birds that day, but the experience had been hot. And when things fizzled out not long after—Morgan had wanted something kinkier than Gael could provide—it had been amicable enough that they still remained friends on social media.

Finally, Gael cleared his throat and called out: "Morgan?"

She looked up from her phone, grinned, and ran over to hug him. He embraced her back. She smelled like citrus lotion and bug spray—same as on their birding trip—and the smell activated something in him. But now wasn't the time to focus on that.

The rest of the group hurried behind Morgan. Gael counted a dozen people. *Jesus, so many people.* He didn't recognize any of them except for Morgan. Was this how all activist groups worked? Churn, burn, and replace, save those consistent few members.

"I swear to God," Morgan whispered, "if that post was a joke, I'm going to be pissed."

She winked at him, as if trying to keep the mood light, but her eyes conveyed a certain desperation.

A moment later, she noticed Maya and smiled.

"You two dating now?" Morgan asked, playfully nudging Gael in the ribs.

Maya stood to greet Morgan. "In his dreams," she said, bringing her in for a hug.

A moment later, Morgan stepped back and looked between Maya and Gael. "Been a minute," she said. "A long one."

"Yup," Gael replied, his mouth suddenly dry. He wasn't sure if Morgan was grateful to see them after years away or pissed that they'd disconnected so completely. Maybe both.

"So, uh, what..." Morgan said, squinting as if searching for her question's end. "What you two been up to all this time?"

Gael glanced at Maya, unsure where to start or perhaps embarrassed to start at all. What did he have to show for after all these years? Maya didn't seem eager to launch into a big update either, her gaze averted.

"Come on, I'm not gonna bite," Morgan said. "Things don't have to be weird, okay?"

The rest of the Earth Unity Alliance members chattered behind Morgan, and one piped up with a question: "Hey, where'd you see the woodpecker?"

Looking more closely at the group, Gael saw people who reminded him of his younger, more engaged self. Most were in their early twenties, but a couple folks were older than Gael by at least a decade. So many environmental activists burnt out, got arrested, or left organizing for job and family obligations. The ones who persisted for years and years were rare. What was their secret? Gael would ask them if he got the chance.

"Okay, so, we'll show you the bird," he said, "but don't get too close, alright? We don't want to scare it."

Maya flashed Gael a quick look—one that said, *Don't make them suspicious*—but he didn't need the reminder.

The activists huddled around him and Maya as they guided them toward the tree. Some whispered with breathless excitement while others stayed perfectly silent, as if even a single sound might jeopardize their chance to see the woodpecker.

"Let's wait here," Maya said, then pointed at the nest. None of the fledglings poked their faces out. "The parent should be back soon."

The activists went dead silent, raising their binoculars and locking them on the tree. Some of their hands shook, struggling to hold steady. At least one person looked on the verge of passing out from sheer anticipation. The rush of wind and the not-so-distant buzz of a saw filled the group's silence.

Gael's neck felt hot and prickly. What if the woodpecker returned with a recognizably human piece of meat? Would everyone notice, or would they be too shocked at the bird's existence to register it?

When the bird flew into view a minute later, clutching an indiscernible chunk of flesh, the group erupted, some gasping in ecstatic disbelief and one even fainting.

Gael's fear of the body being discovered melted away, and in its place flooded a feeling like collective transcendence. He hadn't been part of a church congregation in years, and even when he was, it had never made him feel this close to something holy. But the woodpecker was this group's angel, their salvation, their call to action. And these people—Maya and Morgan and the others he didn't yet know—were united in this struggle for the future.

———◦———

Maya wasn't sure how it happened—if Morgan had called the group to action or if everyone had made the choice collectively—but soon they were marching toward the logging operation with confrontational intent. Maya and Gael followed a few steps behind as the activists waded through thick patches of poison oak, heedless of the pain.

Maya wanted to know which other actions the group had performed in her absence: sit-ins at ecologically vulnerable sites? Animal jailbreaks at fur farms? The doomer in her knew these actions were a drop in the bucket against an encroaching ecopocalypse, and it took effort to dig up that weaker voice of hope buried deep inside her. She had to remind herself that every action, no matter how small, rippled outward. And when many hands joined together, those ripples could reach far shores. Still, that ugly cynicism rose like bile in her throat, and it took only a moment to recognize where it came from: shame. The criticisms she had of her own ineffectual nonprofit work, projected outward. If Earth Unity Alliance's actions were equally ineffectual, she'd have less to feel ashamed about, right? No, it was a stupid, self-centered thought.

Ahead, one of the activists started up a chant: "When our planet's under attack, we stand up and we fight back!" Surely the loggers would hear them coming now; the cops wouldn't be far behind.

Ignore that hopeless bitch in your head and be part of something bigger than yourself.

"We should probably join in," Maya whispered to Gael, stepping over a crumbling snake hole.

Gael's pace slowed, his march becoming a tentative shuffle.

"Don't judge me for this," he said, "but I'm fucking scared. If the cops show up, they're going to find out everything."

"They won't," Maya said, grabbing his trembling hand and leading him forward. She knew her comment wasn't helpful, but she didn't know what else to say. Comforting people had never been one of her talents.

"I don't have a job, I don't have any prospects, and I probably don't have a future," Gael said. His words came out thin, as if he were halfway to a panic attack.

Maya scrambled for something to bring her friend back to earth. "You have purpose right this second," she said. "And you have me. I've got your back, whatever happens."

Was that true though? Just yesterday, she'd failed him at a critical moment.

"I guess we *are* body disposal buddies," Gael said between deep breaths.

Maya laughed and squeezed his hand. "That's right. Just don't talk about it too loud, okay?"

"Oh, trust me, I won't."

Maya closed her eyes for a moment and tried to muster her best self. The version not ruled by ego and pessimism and self-isolation. This moment demanded that version of her, and she wouldn't let anyone down this time.

"Chant with me?" she asked Gael.

"Okay," Gael said.

They joined the others, loud as they could. One activist looked back and smiled; another nodded at them with a dead-serious expression.

And Maya felt it swelling in her chest: purpose and solidarity. It had been ages since she'd last truly experienced it. This march—whatever it would become—felt different from her work at home. It felt right and true.

Chapter 6

Gael was surprised that the logging operation didn't stop when the activists marched to the forest's edge, chanting at the top of their lungs. Maybe the company didn't see them as a threat—just a bunch of naïve tree huggers who the cops would deal with shortly.

A few workers stared at the group from their rumbling vehicles, some with blank expressions and others with smirking amusement. A tall, muscular man who appeared to be their supervisor yelled over the chanting and gestured for the work to continue. All Gael heard was something about quotas.

One of the vehicles resumed its task of severing a tree at the trunk and grasping its prize in metal claws. Morgan broke from the chanting and ran to the vehicle. She was barely taller than its massive treads, but regardless, she screamed at the man inside: "Shut that shit off!"

Morgan still possessed the same shocking boldness Gael had witnessed—and been so attracted to—years ago. Maybe he'd been too meek and mild for her then, but he hoped he wouldn't disappoint her now. More than that, he hoped he wouldn't disappoint himself.

The chants gradually diminished as the group changed tactics. Several activists pulled chains from their backpacks and got to work locking themselves to the trees. One of the workers laughed and shook his head.

Gael didn't have any chains of his own and felt paralyzed, unsure how to be most useful. In truth, he still wanted to hide himself away, escape notice for as long as possible. But he wouldn't do that.

Nearby, the supervisor had a phone pressed to one ear and a finger plugged in the other. Almost certainly calling the cops. The man's face was red with sunburn or anger, probably both.

An idea popped into Gael's head.

"Maya, come with me," he said. "Help me talk to him."

"Why would we do that?" Maya asked.

"We could show him the woodpecker video, mention Endangered Species Act violations, remind him of all those fines the company would incur with any further logging. Make it about money."

"I honestly don't think he'll give a shit about the bird. Or even the fines, really. If you're rich enough, a fine is just a business expense."

"I know, but we need to do *something*."

Maya paused, then nodded. Maybe she, like Gael, understood how committing to an action—even a potentially useless one—was preferable to terror and paralysis.

As soon as Gael ran up to the supervisor, the man dropped his phone and pointed a burled finger at him.

"You're on private fucking property," the supervisor said. "And you'll be headed to prison real soon. Get any closer and I'll make sure it's a long, long sentence."

Gael grabbed Maya's hand as he backed away. The supervisor didn't blink, his wide, white-eyed gaze locked on the two of them.

"Okay, change of plans," Maya whispered to her friend as she took out her phone. "I'll livestream what's happening. If these people have eyes on them, anything they do—"

The supervisor closed the distance between them, snagged Maya's phone out of her hand, and stomped it once, twice, three times under his boot. When he lifted his foot, the screen had been reduced to crystalline spiderwebs.

"Fuck," Maya said.

Gael's body felt frozen, and he hated that this was his reaction to bullies. To freeze when they hurt him or his friends, as if those assholes might mistake him for a statue and lose interest.

Behind Gael, locks clinked and chains rattled. A few activists cheered, joyful in their resistance. Their energy emboldened Gael, melting away his fear. He jabbed a finger at the supervisor.

"You're a piece of shit, you know that?" he said. "You don't get to treat my friend like that, and you don't get to—"

The man put two massive hands on Gael's chest and pushed him to the ground. "When will these fucking cops get here?"

Gael's heart thudded, fierce and angry. He imagined one of the logging vehicles running the supervisor down, the man's flesh caught among the rocks and dirt clods. He imagined the woodpecker swooping in for its sacrificial meal.

Maya's voice tore Gael from the fantasy: "How fucking dare you."

Maya pushed the supervisor back, but the man was built like the trees he destroyed; he barely budged. His reaction was immediate: a slap across Maya's face. She recoiled and clutched her chin.

"Shut up, you dumb cunt," the supervisor said. "Now go back to your trust fund daddy."

The activists screamed at the man, but they could do little to stop him while chained to the trees. Morgan was still free though, and she rushed over to help.

Gael staggered to his feet and considered the odds. With him, Maya, and Morgan, they could probably take the supervisor down, but if the other workers got out of their vehicles to stop them...

Again, the threat of prison haunted Gael. With each passing second, the possibility seemed more and more likely. He felt like throwing up.

But there was no time to dwell on that now. He needed to act.

Wordlessly, he, Morgan, and Maya closed in on the supervisor from three different sides. He didn't know what they'd do to him, but again, he fantasized about violence. Stomping the man's face in like he'd stomped Maya's phone. Leaving a cerebral pulp for the spirits to enjoy.

"Don't fucking touch me," the supervisor said.

But before the three could even get to him, sirens blared. A line of a dozen cop cars zipped up the logging road, red and blue lights flashing.

Within seconds of the cars screeching into the logging camp, the cops launched their attack. Their captain addressed the protestors through a megaphone: "This is an illegal demonstration. Unchain yourselves and do not resist arrest." The rest of the squad drew their police batons and advanced on the group. Some cops ambled forward with bored, distant gazes, as if they'd rather be at home watching ESPN, while others rushed in with bloodthirsty eagerness.

Maya felt paralyzed. She'd been to plenty of protests where people got arrested, but that had been years ago. Nowadays, she'd grown accustomed to protests organized by the nonprofit, never threatening enough to warrant more than one bored cop watching from the sidelines. In fact, part of her job was letting the police know about these demonstrations far in advance like a good little citizen. There, Maya and her coworkers would stand in the sanctioned free speech zone in front of the Capitol building with picket signs—"save wild spaces" and "make America green again"—chanting and listening to speeches for an hour or so before going home. Nothing had ever come from these protests, at least as far as Maya could tell.

Maybe this one would be different. She tried hard to believe it.

The closer the officers got, the more she wanted to run. But no—she needed to stand strong with Gael, Morgan, and the others. She wouldn't forgive herself if she froze up again. Still, she didn't want to get arrested if she could avoid it. She backed up toward the tree line, closer to the chained protestors, never once taking her eyes off the cops. Gael and Morgan followed.

"What should we do?" Maya asked.

"Protect the others," Morgan said. "And don't make the cops' jobs easy."

Whether Morgan meant a physical fight or a figurative one, Maya couldn't tell, but she imagined a police baton smashing in her skull. A psychic throb pulsed down her spine like she'd actually been attacked. Her heart pounded and her adrenaline soared. She had to do something with this energy.

Behind her, the chained protestors booed and jeered and cursed at the cops. When Maya peeked at the other activists, a few looked ready to shit themselves, but a couple seemed genuinely fearless—or were at least good at pretending. Maybe she could channel their nerve.

"Fuck off and quit your jobs!" she shouted at the cops.

Those words drew one of them toward her, and immediately, her terror returned. Before the man could even close the distance, he raised his baton and said, "You're under arrest. Don't resist!"

Maya stepped backward, then stumbled on a tree root, falling on her ass. The cop sped forward, but Morgan intercepted him, spreading her arms out, wide and protective. Gael swooped in to help Maya up.

"Out of the way, bitch!" the cop said, and when Morgan didn't move, he swung on her. Morgan tried to shield herself, but the baton cracked against her skull. She collapsed immediately, and her head hit the ground with equal force. Blood gushed from the split on her scalp. She didn't move.

Maya felt that psychic ache even stronger than before. *An injury to one is an injury to all*, she thought. And now she knew what type of fight this really was.

"I'm gonna fucking kill him," she told Gael, but her friend held her back.

"We don't have anything to fight with."

"I know, but—"

Before Maya could finish the thought, the cop charged her and Gael, baton raised and ready. Maya ducked just in time to avoid the blow, then stomped the cop's knee in with all her might. The man let out a cry and crumpled. Maya didn't wait for him to get to his feet; she knew her hit had been a lucky one and she didn't want to tempt fate. Grabbing Gael's hand, she ran to Morgan.

At the same time, the other cops advanced on the chained protestors, ready for war. They made no effort to unchain and arrest them, instead beating them senseless. Protestors thrashed to escape their chains and shield themselves as the blows rained down. One strike flattened a protestor's nose, and another sent a protestor's tooth flying. Maybe the cops figured it'd be easier to haul them away when they were all like Morgan—unconscious and barely breathing.

"Jesus fucking Christ," Maya said, grabbing Morgan's left arm. "Gael, can you—?"

Without another word, Gael lifted Morgan by her other arm. They needed to haul her somewhere safe and, if at all possible, help a few of the other protestors escape, too.

I hope someone's filming this, Maya thought, quickly followed by another thought: *And I hope whoever watches it actually gives a shit.*

The cop Maya had kicked was limping toward her, reaching for the taser on his belt.

A quick glance to the side revealed that one protestor had escaped her chains and was working to free the others. She would have to do it herself.

"Let's go," Maya said.

She and Gael ran into the woods with Morgan passed out and bobbing between them. The cop's taser crackled behind them, failing to connect with its target. However, the other cops found theirs. More protestors screamed and cursed and pled, but Maya didn't have time to help. Would the others be in a prison cell the next time she saw them? A pine box?

The farther she and Gael ran, the more her heart felt like a ball of lead. She wanted to sob. She wanted to destroy. She wanted to kill. To crush each and every one of these cops and capitalists into a paste.

Yes, killing is what she wanted most of all.

And as the pursuing cop's footfalls faded behind her and the woodpecker's nest grew closer, Maya knew what had to be done.

Chapter 7

After carrying Morgan to camp through thick foliage with a cop in pursuit, Gael felt like his muscles were melting. At least he and Maya had lost the limping officer a few minutes back, so they could rest here a while. They wouldn't have long, but he'd take what time he could get.

Breathing hard and blinking away the sting of sweat, he sat outside the tent with Maya. Morgan lay on the sleeping bag inside, no longer bleeding from the head but still unconscious. Given how much she'd been jostled around, it worried Gael that she hadn't woken up.

"You okay?" Maya asked, grabbing his hand.

Gael squeezed hers in return, a tenderness welling up inside him. Tears and sweat met at the corners of his eyes.

"Never been better," he said, offering a half smile.

Maya laughed, then leaned her head against his.

"I know you're joking, but part of me actually feels that way," she said. "Everything I've done these past few years has felt meaningless, but this could be different. I mean, it fucking sucks, but at least we're doing something. Protecting something worth protecting, for however long we can."

Gael nodded, stroking Maya's hand. Her body was warm and sticky against his, but the closeness felt comforting. How long had it been since someone last touched him? He'd experienced that closeness with Morgan all those years back, but after becoming a teacher, he had a long drought of physical connection. God, he'd missed it.

"I don't think we can stay very long," he said. "Look at how she's breathing."

Morgan's chest rose and fell at an unpredictable rhythm. It reminded Gael of how his dad used to sleep—ragged apneic breaths, sometimes half a minute apart.

"You're probably right," Maya said, wincing as she got to her feet. "We should get her to a hospital."

Gael couldn't tell if he imagined it, but a light seemed to drain from Maya's face. Maybe she didn't want to leave this place that had given her purpose, even if it meant saving someone.

"We can come back, you know?" Gael said. "I mean, if we don't get arrested."

"Can I show you something first? It'll be quick."

Before Gael could answer, Maya walked toward the woodpecker's tree. As she did, something fluttered above. Not the parent, but a fleshed-out fledgling taking flight. Two of its siblings followed, flapping around the tree in clumsy patterns. Gael felt breathless.

"That wasn't what I was going to show you," Maya said, "but holy shit."

"Yeah."

"Here, we'll look at them in a sec. Come over to the trunk and press your ear to it."

Gael did as Maya said, the bark scratching against his cheek. The sound was subtle at first, but it built into something deafening. A thousand ethereal beaks hammering the wood, desperate to get out. Uncountable spirits who could soon find life if presented with the right sacrifice. Gael imagined the fledglings above joined by a legion of siblings, all fed on gifts of human flesh left at their altar, joyfully released from the prison of extinction. The noise was almost overwhelming, and he pulled his ear away.

"Why didn't you tell me earlier?" he asked.

"I don't know," Maya said. "One insane thing at a time, I guess?"

"Goddamn ... I can't even imagine how many there are."

From the tent came a groan. Morgan was waking up. Gael and Maya rushed over, crouching beside the open flap. Morgan's eyes struggled to focus on either of them, and she blinked hard like she was trying to clear away a persistent, obscuring fog.

"Morgan, hey, hey," Gael said, tapping her shoulder. "How are you feeling?"

Morgan's head rotated slowly, as if she were unable to stop its motion, and she didn't seem to register Gael's question right away. Only after he tapped her again did she respond.

"No, I don't have feelings for you," she said, then turned to puke all over Maya's sleeping bag.

"That's not—" Gael started, but he knew it was pointless in Morgan's current state. He turned his attention to Maya and whispered, "We need to get her out of here now."

"Okay," Maya said, deadpan.

"Listen," Gael said, lifting Morgan onto his right shoulder and motioning at Maya. "Just help me get her to my car, and—and you can stay here if you want to. I'll drive her to the hospital, and you can protect the nest."

While Maya grabbed Morgan's other side, a dark glint lit up her eyes. "Protection isn't enough," she said. "We need to go farther."

Gael knew what she meant but said nothing, instead starting the trek back toward his car. Morgan groaned, hanging mostly limp between him and Maya. Gael's legs ached under the weight. If the cops caught them on the way back—or ambushed them by the car—he didn't know if he'd be able to run. Hopefully, adrenaline would do its miraculous work.

———

The farther they got from the nest, the more Maya worried about the birds. What if something happened to them while she was away? Or what if she got arrested and lost her chance to bring more of them back? She'd rather die.

No, I'd rather kill.

The cops were still nearby; she could sense it. No chance they'd leave before catching the woman who fucked up an officer's knee. If she saw them, she'd find one way or another to feed them to the birds.

She'd spent so many years sitting in board meetings with people who would've been better off as bird food. Donors wealthier than God who pretended to be nature's greatest stewards. But no one got that rich without shedding the blood of the world. Billionaires, bosses, and cops—the lot of them belonged down a woodpecker's gullet.

And maybe other gullets as well: from somewhere in the forest came a guttural howl, distinctly animal but also ethereal, yearning. Maya thought back to the large chunks torn from the old man's corpse, to the sounds she'd sensed just below the surface of perception when she'd entered these woods. The woodpeckers weren't the only extinct creatures devouring their way back to life. Whether this howling creature was a wolf—long since hunted out of existence in this area of the world—or a beast even more ancient, she had no way of knowing.

"Any idea what bird that is?" Gael asked, panting as he helped Maya heft Morgan over a fallen tree.

Maya laughed. No matter how angry she was, she could think of no one better to be in this mess with. She only hoped Gael would do what was necessary when the time came. With any luck, they'd be able to take out the cops and still get Morgan the care she needed.

And then she heard it—her chance to do exactly that. Somewhere not far off, heavy footfalls and raised voices echoed through the trees: "Stop, or I'll shoot!" followed by "Fuck, fuck, fuck!"

Maya recognized the second voice—one of the protestors who'd jeered at the cops while chained to a tree.

Gael ducked, but Maya stayed up. She shrugged Morgan off her shoulder, easing her to the ground, and drew out her pocket knife. Unfolding the blade, she imagined where she'd stick it. *No body armor on the neck*.

Gael gave her a wide-eyed look—one that suggested he'd known this was coming but didn't realize it would be so soon. Maya only hoped he was ready.

She nodded at him, and after a moment, he swallowed hard and nodded back. He rested the motionless Morgan against the trunk of a tree, whispered something in her ear, and then drew out his multitool, unfolding its blade.

Good, Maya thought. And she began her pursuit.

Another series of sounds broke through, closer now: cracking branches, the *thud* of a body hitting dirt, and a metallic jangle. Maya crept forward and took in the scene.

The cop was on top of the protestor, a young black man, pressing him into the ground and trying to wrestle on a pair of handcuffs.

"Stay fucking still," the cop said.

"That ... hurts," the protestor grunted, his voice muffled in a pile of leaves.

The cop hammered a closed fist on the back of his head. The protestor let out a cry and squirmed, unable to escape the pin.

Neither one noticed Maya or Gael as they approached from behind. When Maya looked to her friend, she saw in his eyes a bloodshot fury, and she knew then that they were on the same page about what they had to do. She pointed at him, motioned to the left, and then counted down from five on her hand.

At zero, they advanced from opposite sides. When Gael reached the cop, he wrapped his arms around the man's head and squeezed as hard as he could. Simultaneously, Maya plunged her knife into the cop's neck once, twice, three times, blood jetting from each new hole.

The cop's scream became a gurgle, and Maya stopped stabbing. Gael locked eyes with her and communicated his resolve soundlessly. Still squeezing the cop's draining head, he took a deep breath, closed his eyes, and drove his knife into the man's temple. The cop seized, every muscle in his body stiffening, and then collapsed limp in Gael's grip. Before he could fall onto the protestor, Maya and Gael guided the leaking corpse into the brush.

Voice shaking, Gael said, "Hope the woodpeckers and, uh ... whatever the hell else is out here find him before the other cops do."

Maya gripped Gael's hands, breathing heavily, the intensity of what they'd done igniting every nerve in her body. Gael shuddered and closed his eyes.

"Oh no," the protestor said. He was sitting upright now, massaging the back of his head and looking at his dead attacker.

Maya shifted her attention to the man. "Hey, it's okay. You didn't do that. It was—"

"I'm covered in his blood," he said, wringing the cop's life from the back of his shirt. "Fuck."

"Don't worry about it," Maya said, reaching out her hand. "We'll get you—"

"Don't touch me. I—I'm not going to prison for something I didn't do."

"Okay, well, let's get you out of here then. Back home." Guilt jolted through Maya as she remembered her grandmother at home and considered the possibility that she might not be returning to care for her after all this. Suddenly, those countless nights spent changing Jolene's diapers and spooning her soft food and watching cooking competition shows with her in complete silence sounded like the greatest thing in the world. "Gael and I will clean up this mess."

As if on cue, six fledgling woodpeckers zipped through the trees and dove toward the cop's corpse. Three of them tore flesh from the stab wounds in his neck, and the other three busied themselves by pecking through the dark blue fabric of his slacks. The birds swallowed great chunks—likely more weight than their wings could carry—and spewed up silvery-blue ooze after each bite, ejecting the ethereal to make room for the physical.

"Holy fuck," the protestor said.

"Hey, what's your name?" Gael asked as he backtracked a few steps and hefted Morgan back onto his shoulder. He grunted and bit his lip, trembling.

"Cody," the protestor said. "Is she okay?"

"Not really," Gael said. "She needs a hospital. Do you think you could help?"

Cody stumbled to his feet, hesitating before answering. Finally, he said, "Yeah, of course."

"Thanks," Gael said. "We'll help get her to the road. Maya?"

Maya held up a finger, then tentatively approached the cop's corpse. The birds didn't move at first, and she worried that if she startled them, they might fly off or even peck at her. But they continued on with their meal, unbothered, beaks clacking and wings rustling in the gore. Maybe they recognized that she'd made this sacrifice for them—that she was a friend, not a meal. Eventually, the flock might be big and strong enough to hunt humans themselves, but that time had not yet come.

From somewhere nearby came another otherworldly howl. Whatever the beast was, Maya didn't want to wait and find out.

She grabbed the taser and pepper spray from the cop's belt, and Gael snagged the gun. The woodpeckers shifted to make room for her, as if she might join in their feast. She wouldn't stay, but if they were lucky, she and Gael would be the chef of their next meal, too.

Chapter 8

Gael expected the forest's sounds to dwindle the closer they got to the road, but the opposite was true. The woodpecker fledglings trumpeted in their squeaky juvenile way, and other birds—sparrows and buntings and flickers—greeted them like old friends reunited at last. Somewhere close, that other creature yowled, and another of its kind yowled back. It was as if the cop's death had awoken something that refused to be contained to this small sliver of wilderness—not after so many years spent in the limbo of extinction. Humans loved to enclose nature, to section it off from civilization with fences and borders and industrial violence. But nature always resisted, sometimes in small ways—a moth squeezing into a windowsill—and sometimes in bigger ones. Whatever was unfolding now seemed big. Gael only hoped these creatures would continue to tolerate his presence.

"Hold up," Maya whispered as they neared the road. "I hear cars. Could be cops."

Gael instinctively checked his belt loop for the gun, as if it had always been a part of him and not something he'd stolen off a corpse mere minutes ago. Then he glanced at Morgan, still hanging limp from his and Maya's shoulders. She looked pale as birch bark. Whether her bleeding had been purely external or internal too, Gael couldn't say. He only hoped they'd have enough time to save her. Maybe if they both survived this, they could meet up again. Reconnect, if not romantically, then as friends. But there'd be time to dream about that later.

"Cody, where'd you park?" Gael asked.

"I tried to hide my car off the road, but you can kind of see it from here," Cody said, pointing somewhere just beyond the tree line.

Gael squinted into the brush for a few seconds before he spotted it. The old rusted beater looked perfectly at home in the ditch, as if that's where it was meant to be. It reminded him of his old car.

Tilting his head, he listened for cops, but hearing anything was difficult over the chatter of birds. Perhaps the woodpeckers were sharing stories from the afterlife—or begging for their next meal.

Gael didn't enjoy feeding them—he'd never wanted to kill anyone, not seriously—but he knew he wouldn't hesitate next time. Not if the person in front of him had a badge and a gun.

"I think we're safe," he said. "Let's load Morgan in and go."

"Are you coming, too?" Cody asked, his eyes wide and nervous. Maybe he still carried the dream of a normal life after this, and the thought of transporting two cop killers jeopardized it.

But Gael wouldn't do that to him. As long as Maya was here, he'd be here, too. They still had work to do.

"Okay, come on," Maya said.

Gael moved in sync with Maya, trying not to jostle Morgan around. When they reached the car, Cody crouched to unlock it. Gael loaded Morgan in, laying her across the seat and making sure she'd be safe and comfortable. Part of him was sure she wouldn't make it to the hospital. She'd die at a stoplight, or die when the cops pulled Cody over, or die when the car sputtered its last and died along with her. But there was a chance she'd survive, however slight. Maybe Morgan and Cody would get away and live free lives. Gael squeezed Morgan's hand once, the shape of her still so familiar after all these years.

"They'll come," Morgan muttered, her eyes still closed. "If we let them in. Like a big old party. Not just here. They'll be—ooh."

She turned to the side, dry heaved, and went silent once more.

Uncertain what to make of Morgan's words, Gael said, "I'll buy you a drink when this is all over," then closed the door.

Cody hopped into the driver's seat and tried starting the car. The ignition proved just as aged as the rest of the vehicle, failing once, twice, three times, before finally starting on the fourth.

"Well, this whole thing has been incredible and absolutely fucked," Cody said to Gael and Maya through the open window. "I don't know if I'll ever see you two ag—"

Before he could finish, a cop car whipped around the curve of the road, heading in the group's direction.

Gael froze like a scared rabbit for a moment, then came to his senses and slapped the hood of the car.

"Go, go, go!"

Cody zipped out of the ditch and onto the road with surprising speed. Gael pictured Morgan bouncing around in the back, and he wished then that he'd buckled her up. Too late now.

The cop car flashed its lights, whooped its sirens, and began its pursuit. But Gael wouldn't let that happen. Morgan and Cody had to get out safe. Without another thought, he ran into the road, waving his arms.

"What are you doing?" Maya asked.

Gael didn't answer, and Maya didn't follow, at least not yet.

When Gael reached the road, the cop car screeched to a halt in front of him with a spray of gravel. He blinked the dust out of his eyes and prepared for whatever might happen next.

A cop lurched out of the car, hands hovering over his gun.

"Get on the fucking ground," he said.

Gael hadn't thought this far ahead. What would he do if he actually got arrested? For now, he held up his hands and slowly squatted.

"Oh, shit," the cop said, pushing a button on his walkie while drawing his weapon. "Suspect on the east road has a gun. I repeat, suspect—"

"Hey, shithead!"

Maya's shout jolted the cop's attention away, and immediately the man fired shot after shot into the brush. When Maya dropped out of sight, the cop spun back toward Gael, losing his grip on the gun in the process.

Gael didn't have time to see if Maya had been hit. This would be his one chance. Pulling out the gun, he fired twice. One shot blew off the cop's ear, and the other bored a hole through his cheek. The man collapsed, writhing and bleeding profusely. A few more spasms and he went still. A voice blared through his walkie, increasingly intense, asking if he was still there.

Gael ran to the ditch, praying Maya was okay. He couldn't find her at first, looking left and right and all around until he spotted her laying down, buried in tangled foliage. Maya sucked sharp breaths through tight lips, clutching a patch of dark red on her upper right arm.

"Hey, talk to me," Gael said, searching himself for anything he could use to stop the bleeding.

"You got him, right?" Maya said, smiling even as her face spasmed. "Where'd you learn how to ... fucking shit ... shoot like that?"

Gael tore off his shirt and tied it around the wound. Not the most sanitary solution, but it would have to do.

"You remember those arcade games at the mall?" he said, his voice trembling. "I got real good at the dino hunter one with the fake plastic gun."

"Close enough to the real thing, I guess." Maya closed her eyes and took a few slow, deep breaths before speaking again. "Can you count down from five and then help me up?"

"Of course," Gael said, grabbing her hand on her uninjured side. "Five, four—"

From the road came the sound of something scraping against gravel. Worried the cop might still be alive, Gael turned just in time to see the cop's corpse being dragged into the brush, then into the forest. A dense honeysuckle bush prevented Gael from clearly seeing what had dragged him, but whatever it was, it was big. He thought again about those unseen howling things and wondered which forgotten corner of natural history they'd been resurrected from. A flock of a dozen ivory-billed woodpeckers flitted behind the corpse, eager for whatever scraps the larger creature would leave behind.

Without finishing the countdown, Gael pulled Maya to her feet. She stumbled a few steps, then grabbed him by the arm, steadying herself.

"Let's go back by the tree line," she said. "Try to lure in some more cops as they come down the road."

"You sure?" Gael asked. "You're pretty fucked up. We could come back when—"

"You know we're not going to get another chance."

"Yeah." Gael was silent for a moment, thinking about the future he'd lost, the future everyone left could gain if only he and Maya made a few more sacrifices. He wasn't sure how many more times they'd get lucky in a fight with a cop, but they'd have to try.

"You think that cop's gun still has any rounds?" Maya asked, pointing to the weapon left on the road.

"I don't know. He really tried to kill you there. Glad he's a mediocre shot." Gael ran to the road and grabbed the pistol. He checked the clip—still a couple rounds left. Better than nothing.

Rejoining Maya, he offered an arm for support, but she shrugged him off.

"I'm good," she said. "But if I bleed through your shirt, can I have your pants?"

Gael grinned even as a lump formed in his throat. He felt like crying.

As they entered the forest once more, it sounded more alive than even a few minutes back, the chatter of birds and yowling of not-so-distant beasts building to a frenzy. Just a few corpses had gone a long way. Was it only three, though? What if the cops had killed some of the protestors and the forest had consumed them? Or what if the creatures were hunting humans themselves now? Gael shuddered.

Soon, they found a place hidden from the road but close enough that they'd be able to hear any cop cars. Gael pointed out a mossy boulder for Maya to rest on, but she shook her head. However, only a few seconds passed before she let out a hiss of pain and leaned her good arm against the rock. The shirt bandage was nearly soaked through, and Maya looked a shade or two paler than normal.

"Come on, just lay down," Gael said, guiding her into a sitting position. Maya plopped onto the boulder, then rested her head in its mossiest pocket. "I'll let you know when something's happening."

Maya said nothing and closed her eyes, but it didn't seem like she was too out of it to understand him. Rather, she appeared to be tuning into something else, pressing her ear deeper into the boulder's divot.

"How's your Tempur-Pedic?" Gael asked.

"Shhh," Maya said.

Several seconds of silence followed, and even the creatures of the forest ceased their chatter, as if they too wanted to know what Maya was hearing.

Whatever was happening, Gael didn't like it. He'd encountered people close to death several times, and they always did strange things leading up to their final breath. His dad had spoken to his long-dead mother in the minutes before he passed. Hopefully Maya's behavior had a different explanation.

When she finally opened her eyes and spoke, she did so with a smile.

"There are more of them," she said. "I have no idea what they are, but they're not woodpeckers and they're not ... whatever that other thing is. We can bring them back to life for the first time in thousands, millions of years. There are so many hungry spirits, Gael. I can hear them crawling in the moss, scratching under the rocks, burrowing in the dirt. Everywhere. Listen..."

Gael knelt beside Maya, noticing sticky blood droplets in the moss. He'd need to change her bandage soon. Maya barely seemed to care, bliss shining through her drained complexion. Pressing his ear to the stone, Gael listened. The sensation was cool and soothing against his cheek, but he heard nothing save for his pulse thumping in his ear. The seconds stretched into a minute, and still there was only a mountain of silence.

"I ... I don't hear anything," he said, his throat catching.

"But they're so loud," Maya said. "How—oh, they're hungry, Gael. They need our help."

Maybe Maya was close enough to death that she could sense the other side. Sure, both she and Gael had been able to see the woodpeckers, but maybe those birds had always been closer to this world than the next, still fresh in the human imagination. Maybe the others Maya heard—whatever they were—had long been lost to memory, drifting further and further into the void.

"God, you're bleeding a lot," Gael said. Taking off his belt, he started work on a tighter makeshift tourniquet.

"I was kidding about needing your pants," Maya said, her words slurring. A delirious sort of happiness fuzzed the edge of each syllable.

Gael removed the blood-soaked shirt. Maya winced but otherwise barely seemed to register what was happening, too tuned in to the world of invisible spirits. Gael tried tying his belt around her arm, but the leather was too stiff to cooperate. His pants would have to do. Stripping them off, he quickly tied the legs just above the wound. Maya's bleeding slowed to a trickle—probably as good as it would get for now.

"Morgan wasn't crazy," Maya said.

"What do you mean?" Gael asked.

"She sensed them too. That's why she was saying those weird things. It's why—"

"Maya? Hey, you okay?" Gael snapped his fingers in front of her face, which had taken on an expression somewhere between blankness and pure focus.

"They're everywhere, Gael. Not just here. They're in the city, they're in—"

"Who's 'they'?"

"I ... I don't know yet. But they want to come back. They miss the world they had. We just have to look and listen for them, and then—you know. I ... I think my grandma can sense them, too. I think she wants to really see them before she..."

"Yeah..."

Right then, Gael felt someone or something watching them. Keeping low, he turned his attention from Maya, reached for the pistol, and scanned his surroundings. No more cops on the road just yet. But there, peeking out from behind a giant fallen tree, were two glinting eyes and a huge shaggy shape twice his height. It was cloaked in shadow, but Gael knew this was the same beast that had dragged the dead cop off the road. While he couldn't be certain, he sensed that the animal was prehistoric—some lost terror of the Ice Age.

"Maya," he said. "That howling thing is looking at us."

Maya made no motion to get up. Her face looked peaceful, unbothered.

"We don't have to worry," she said. "It will only take me if I die. If I give myself."

Gael wasn't sure why, but he believed Maya. In her liminal state, she possessed a knowledge he couldn't yet access—at least not without joining her on the precipice of death.

"Okay," he said. His heart pounded as he turned toward the beast once more, and he felt vulnerable in his near-nakedness. Projecting his voice, he addressed the creature. "We'll find you another meal, but it's not going to be her, alright?"

He doubted the beast comprehended his words, but regardless, it slunk away, deeper into the woods.

Then, sirens, close and getting louder.

On cue, Maya pushed herself into a sitting position, swaying with dizziness. She reached for Gael as her eyes rolled back involuntarily. "Give me one of the guns."

"I know you want to help," Gael said, "but there's no way you'll be able to do that right now."

"That's fair. I—" Before Maya could finish her sentence, she tilted her head and winced, her whole body quivering. "Fuck."

The sirens let out one last *whoop* as two cop cars skidded to a stop on the road. Four cops burst out of the doors, weapons drawn, scanning their surroundings.

"Where'd Jason go?" one asked. "He even radioed—"

"Oh, what the fuck," another said. He pressed a button on his walkie, and it blooped. "Uhh, officer down, I think. No body, but a lot of blood. It could be from one of the protestors, but I can't be sure."

"I hope it is. I'll kill the next one I see."

"Cut that shit out. They're gonna put you on leave again."

"Both of you shut up," the cop with the walkie said. "Keep your guard up and see if you can find him."

"Yes, sir."

Like that, they dispersed. The bloodthirsty cop wandered in Gael and Maya's direction, gun raised, but didn't seem to notice them. Gael grabbed Maya's good arm and dragged her to the forest floor. The nettles stung, but it was loads better than getting shot.

"How many?" Maya asked.

Gael would have shushed her, but her voice was already so faint. No chance the cop would hear her.

"Too many," he said.

He didn't want to lift his head and risk getting caught, so he listened for footsteps. The cop crept closer at first, then farther away. The others checked in through shouts. A distant "find anything?" and a closer "Jason? You there?"

"I don't want us to die," Gael said. "I want to enjoy the world we're making. To spend time in it with you and Morgan and—"

He stalled out there, realizing just how few people he still had in his life.

Maya let out a half-conscious grunt, either in agreement or acknowledgment. The pants around her wound had soaked through with blood, too. Gael wondered what would happen if she died right here. Would that beast and the woodpeckers sense it and come to feast? Would they bring her meat back to their spectral young?

Gael didn't want that. To be alone in this world and scared. Destined for death soon after his friend, right when things were starting to look promising. Maybe this place didn't have to be his last stand. Maybe Maya would forgive him if he took her out of here so they could fight another day. He needed a plan of escape, but so many cops around made it risky.

Just as he wracked his brain for a way out, a bloodcurdling scream echoed from the other side of the road. It raised in pitch and intensity for a few seconds before abruptly cutting off. Maybe a cop had tackled and beat a protestor. Or maybe the resurrected creatures had made their own sacrifice, disemboweling the police captain. Gael hoped it was the latter. And if it was, did he really have to stay here? No, he could go home and enjoy whatever life he had left. God, he was tired.

Yelling, the cops converged on where the screams had come from, guns drawn and ready to fire. Gael waited one minute, two, until their footsteps faded deeper into the forest. Then, he dragged his barely conscious friend toward his car, hoping he wasn't making a mistake.

Chapter 9

Maya opened her eyes. Between the dizziness and blinding light, she couldn't tell where she was. She sensed that she was moving—or that something was moving her—but couldn't otherwise orient herself. The thing moving her turned, and the light's intensity lessened. Its afterimage was seared into her vision, but as the floaters vanished, clouds took their place, framed through the curve of a backseat car window. She'd been staring directly at a sunset without realizing.

When she tried to prop herself into a sitting position, a sharp pain jolted through her right arm. Gael's clothes no longer wrapped her wound, but instead, actual medical bandages. Only a small amount of blood had leaked through. Whether that meant the wound had clotted or Maya was running out of blood, she had no way of knowing.

"You're awake," Gael said, looking at her in the rearview mirror.

His car barrelled down a two-lane highway, bordered by sorghum fields and closer to the city than the forest. Fighting through the fuzziness in her head, Maya guessed they were an hour from home. No siren-blaring cop cars trailed them; they were alone on the road, for now.

"How you feeling?" Gael asked.

"Not great," Maya said, then motioned to her bandages. "Did you do this?"

"Yup. Had a first aid kit in the trunk. Really should have brought it into the forest with us, but my brain was scrambled. I disinfected your wound, too. Didn't want my nasty jeans to give you some sort of swamp ass infection."

"Thanks." Maya would have laughed, but she felt like she'd pass out if she did.

A few seconds of silence passed before Gael spoke again. "I hope you're not pissed that I decided to take us home," he said. "I know we could have done more there, but ... I think the creatures can take care of themselves now. I'm pretty sure that's what the screaming was."

The car made a gentle turn, but the movement was enough to make Maya feel the emptiness inside her body—swirling void where there should have been sloshing blood. She needed something to drink now.

"Do we have any water?" she asked.

Gael grabbed a plastic water bottle from the passenger seat, unscrewed its cap, and passed it back to her. Maya gulped it down in seconds. Even though it had been boiling in the car's summer heat for who knows how long, it was the most refreshing drink she'd ever had.

Immediately, her near-vertigo lessened to just a slight dizziness, and her vision sharpened. She didn't feel on the precipice of death anymore, at least for the moment.

A thought occurred to her then. A test. She looked out the window, squinting into the weeds that hung over the road's shoulder. Would she see or at least sense them lurking there?

The spirits she'd communed with on that mossy boulder? Or perhaps the distant evolutionary cousins of those spirits, long lost to human understanding.

No matter how hard she squinted, she sensed nothing. No strange shapes outlined in the road's rising heat. No feeling of being watched by something beneath the shadows of leafy pigweed.

The further she pulled herself from death, the more the spiritual signal weakened. Still, she knew they were there—the plethora of *them*, whatever they were, from both the Anthropocene and deep, deep in the pre-human past. She knew they would welcome a sacrifice—and, if Gael was right, eventually make sacrifices of their own.

Again, she thought about how Grandma Jolene stared out the window at all hours. Maya had long attributed this behavior to Alzheimer's, but she knew now that her grandmother was sensing something others could not. Something only a closeness to death could peel back and reveal. People in good health had no clue what lay just beneath the surface of their world, buried under a history of human greed and indifference, or even deeper under countless strata of geologic time.

Maya knew where she had to go next. What gift she would give her grandmother.

Gael thought about taking Maya to a hospital, but a gunshot wound would only lead to questions. She seemed stable for the moment; treatment could probably wait.

At Maya's insistence, they drove to her house. Gael didn't like the idea, especially given that the cops could come knocking—or rather, busting in—at any moment. Maya had made it easy to follow their tracks. She'd filmed the livestream that drew in the activists, and she'd left her broken phone at the scene of the protest. It probably wouldn't be long before they traced her home address. Gael couldn't help but feel a little bitter toward his friend. Still, didn't he bear some of the blame? The logging company's trailcam had almost certainly caught him, too. He didn't know if he could cope with being on the run the rest of his life.

But there were bigger problems to deal with—ones that Gael and Maya had unleashed themselves. The car radio offered a glimpse.

"Sorry to interrupt the program, folks," the DJ said, cutting Britney Spears off mid-song, "but police have reported multiple deadly attacks by unknown animals in the area. Citizens are advised to shelter in place. To report any—"

Gael shut off the radio before he could hear any more, his whole body shaking. He glanced at Maya in the rearview, her eyes ringed and haunted.

"Hopefully, they're only eating people who deserve it," she said.

"Yeah," Gael replied, unsure what else to say.

The sky was dark by the time they parked outside the house. No cops or SWAT teams had arrived, probably too preoccupied with animal assailants. Gael got out of the car and helped Maya do the same. She winced but otherwise seemed steady. Her bandages didn't look overly bloody either.

"Of course Brandon's not here," she said, pointing to the empty driveway.

"Some people get deadbeat dads. You got a deadbeat brother," Gael said.

"I'd sure like to beat him dead. Just hope Grandma's okay."

With Maya's good arm draped over Gael's shoulder, they shuffled up the sidewalk to the house. No lights illuminated the interior. Maya unlocked the door, and they stepped inside. Gael felt around for a lightswitch and lit up the foyer.

"Grandma?" Maya asked. "Grandma, you there?"

Before Gael could help Maya into the living room, she hobbled in that direction with urgency. Part of Gael expected to hear her cry out after stumbling upon her grandmother's corpse, but instead Maya breathed a sigh of relief. There Jolene was, sitting in her armchair, staring out the window in the darkened room. Gael turned on a lamp to get a better view. He hadn't seen the woman since before his transition, and the thought that she might not recognize him filled him with an odd mixture of sadness and relief. But Jolene didn't turn and she didn't speak. She just kept staring out the window, silent and lightly breathing. Gael hoped there'd be time for reintroductions later, if the world lasted that long.

"Jesus, Grandma," Maya said. "Brandon could have at least helped you get to bed when it got dark. Asshole."

Still, Jolene said nothing.

Maya glanced at Gael for a moment before dropping her gaze. Something about her expression—dark and serious and secretive—chilled him.

"What's up?" he asked.

"Can you grab me some more bandages?" Maya asked. "Grandma keeps some in the bathroom. Bottom left cabinet."

Gael knew Maya wasn't telling him something, but he nodded and walked toward the bathroom. Even though he hadn't been in this house in years, he still knew where everything was. So little about its setup had changed, from the baby pictures of Maya and Brandon on the walls to the decorative glass orbs on the kitchen windowsill. The house even smelled the same—a smell that could only be compared to itself, as is the case with any treasured home.

While Gael was searching the bathroom cabinet, he froze at the sound of police sirens. They were distant, and after a few seconds of waiting, became even more so. Not for him and Maya. Maybe for someone who'd had their guts ripped out by an ancient howling beast or their eyes pecked to mush by a flock of woodpeckers.

Gael's search had only just resumed when another sound interrupted him. A *chunk* followed by a prolonged shuddering gasp.

Running out of the bathroom, Gael found the sound's source almost immediately. Maya stood in the dimly lit kitchen, a butcher knife in one hand and her chopped-off pinky in the other. The finger's stump spurted once, twice, three times—each weaker than the last.

"Bandages," Maya said, the word a breathless inhale.

Gael ran back into the bathroom, found what he was looking for, and snagged the box. Then, like lightning, he was back in the kitchen, wrapping Maya's oozing stump.

"What the fuck are you doing?" he asked.

"Trust me," she said, her whole body shaking as Gael tightened the bandage. "Done?"

"I fucking guess so. I—seriously, you need to tell me what's going on."

"Watch Grandma. I'll be right back."

"Fine," Gael said. "But then I want answers."

"Don't worry, you'll have them."

Without another word, Maya palmed her severed pinky and stumbled toward the back door.

Maya had never been in this much pain before. It felt like a game of tennis, bouncing between her gunshot wound and severed finger stump, each rally more agonizing than the previous. But it wouldn't last forever, and purpose-fueled adrenaline would carry her through the next few minutes.

Before walking into the backyard, she turned on the outdoor security light. It lit up the parched lawn, the rotted remnants of Grandma's flower garden, and the crabapple tree swaying beside the fence.

It wouldn't matter where she left her pinky. The spirits here—could she see their faint outlines again? Another round of blood loss bringing back her spectral vision?—would find her offering. But she knew her grandmother looked at the tree most often; it's where she was looking right now, a wide-eyed and horrified Gael by her side. Maya placed her pinky in a crook between thick branches, then stepped to the side so she wouldn't block her grandmother's view.

A few seconds went by in which nothing happened, and then Maya saw it. Or at least thought she did. Higher in the tree, a shape—the whisper of a silhouette—hopped down from branch to branch. Perhaps it was only the wind descending to earth, each branch a rung on its ladder, but no, this silhouette had weight to it. Then, the pinky moved. Some near-invisible thing was playing with its food. Another moment passed before, all at once, the pinky disappeared into thin air, down the spirit's gullet. In its place appeared a bird the size of a robin with all the colors of the ocean—shimmering aquamarine feathers intertwined in lapis lazuli depths. It was like nothing Maya—or perhaps any living human—had ever seen before. This bird belonged to a history long forgotten or repressed. But now it belonged to the future, too.

The bird stared at Maya, motionless and expectant. Perhaps it, like the woodpecker, had a nest of its own. A thousand little fledgling souls squeezed between the rings of this crabapple tree, screeching for release. Maybe, when other resurrected beasts converged on the city, this bird would share the spoils of their hunt and bring back its children.

Maya looked toward the window. For the first time in years, her grandmother was smiling, ear to ear, rocking in her chair with as much joy as she could muster. Gael was smiling too, in both awe and horror. Maya would have to apologize to him when she went back inside. And it seemed that time would come sooner than she would've liked.

The wail of sirens echoed into the night, far off but getting closer this time. Even if they weren't for her and Gael, it was time for them to leave. Who knew if the encroaching beasts would recognize and spare them? Had word of her and Gael's sacrifices spread as quickly as the animals themselves? If not, it was best to be cautious.

Maya glanced at the strange bird one more time, smiled, and then headed inside.

———

Gael wasn't sure staying at the house was their safest option, but with each minute that passed, he heard more and more sirens, none of which seemed to be for them. Helicopters joined the commotion, rotors batting at the air while searchlights tracked roving horrors. From one neighborhood over came explosions

of gunfire—perhaps a violent encounter with the animal undead.

"We should board the windows," Gael said.

"Probably," Maya replied. "But can we leave a little gap so
Grandma can watch that bird? I didn't chop off my finger for
nothing."

"You're nuts, you know that? But yeah, of course."

"I'm nuts, but that *is* a spectacular bird."

"Not that you would have known that before you cut your
damn—"

"Yeah, yeah, yeah. Grandma's happy though, so I am, too."

A moment of silence passed between them. Jolene was still
staring out the window, grinning wide as ever at their backyard
visitor. Maya rubbed the woman's shoulders and kissed the top
of her head.

"I love you, Grandma."

Jolene hummed and nodded in return.

Gael flopped onto the couch and closed his eyes. "I need to
rest a bit before we board the place up."

Maya sat beside him, smelling faintly of dirt and iron. "Same.
I'm so fucking tired. I could go for some painkillers, too."

"And I could go for some Chinese food. I'm fucking starving.
Bet no one's delivering tonight though."

"I'd hate it if our driver got—"

"I don't want to think about that."

Outside, not far off now, came the sounds of children screaming and running. Gael hoped it was a nighttime game of tag, but he knew it wasn't.

A shiver ran through him. He needed warmth. Closeness.

"You mind if I put my head in your lap?" he asked. "Rest my eyes for a bit?"

"Of course," Maya said.

In more of a collapse than a controlled descent, Gael laid down. Maya ran the fingers of her good hand through his hair, slow and gentle. Gael's head tingled, a feeling of peace radiating through him. It wouldn't last long, but he'd savor it while it did.

"I'm really glad you invited me on this trip," Maya said.

"I'm so fucking glad you came," Gael replied, tears blurring the edge of his vision.

Whatever terrors came scratching at the door, he was glad to have a friend by his side once more. Someone who'd stay with him until the writhing, verdant end.

Acknowledgements

Corey Farrenkopf

As always, I'd like to thank my friends and family who have been supportive of my writing over the years. It means a lot to me. I'd also like to thank all of the environmental librarians I've worked with, particularly Michelle Eberle and the other Blue Marble Librarians who've worked so hard to help avoid the nightmare scenarios you'll find in this book. And finally, a big thanks to Eric. I was looking for a reason to write this sad weird little story and he gave me the occasion to do so.

Tiffany Morris

A previous version of "A New and Different Hunger" appeared in *Monstroddities* (Sliced Up Press, 2022).

Eric Raglin

Thanks so much to Polly Schattel for your mentorship. I wouldn't have completed this novella without your guidance and encouragement. Thanks to Donyae Coles for the wonderfully thoughtful edits. Thanks to Cozy and Andrew for the sensitivity readings. And thank you, Mom, for fostering my love of birds, without which this novella wouldn't exist.

Content Warnings

The Final Sight: animal death, parent death

"The Neon Dread of Leaves": mass death, suicidal ideation, insects

"A New and Different Hunger": animal death, animal cannibalism

"The Honey Harvest": strangulation

"Looking for the Flower-Man": suicidal ideation

On Phantom Wings: transphobia, racism, misogyny, police brutality, self-harm

About the Authors

Corey Farrenkopf lives on Cape Cod and works as a librarian. His work has been published in Strange Horizons, Electric Literature, Nightmare, Fantasy, The Deadlands, Weird Horror, and elsewhere. He is the author of the novel, Living in Cemeteries, and the short story collection, Haunted Ecologies. To learn more, follow him on Bluesky and Instagram at @Corey-Farrenkopf or on the web at CoreyFarrenkopf.com

Tiffany Morris is an L'nu'skw (Mi'kmaw) writer from Nova Scotia. She is the author of ecohorror novella *Green Fuse Burning* and the horror poetry collection *Elegies of Rotting Stars*. Her work has won Aurora and Elgin Awards and been nominated for the Indigenous Voices Awards, Shirley Jackson Awards, and the Ignyte Awards. Her short stories and poetry have also appeared in the Indigenous horror anthology *Never Whistle At Night*, as well as in *Nightmare Magazine*, *Uncanny Magazine*, and *Apex Magazine,* among others.

Eric Raglin is a horror/Weird fiction writer. His short story collections include *Nightmare Yearnings* and *Extinction Hymns*. He owns Cursed Morsels Press and has edited *The Writhing, Verdant End; No Trouble at All* (co-edited with Alexis DuBon); *Bitter Apples*; *Shredded: A Sports and Fitness Body Horror Anthology*; and *Antifa Splatterpunk*. Find him on Bluesky or Instagram @ericraglin1992.

Other Releases from Cursed Morsels Press

Shaky Pictures of Vanished Faces
by D. Matthew Urban

Budget cuts drive a burned-out humanities professor to master the art of annihilation. A girl on the verge of a transformation seeks out a new member for her isolated, inhuman family. A glitching brain implant shatters its owner's sense of reality. A high-school athlete's body becomes the vessel of a fleshy apocalypse.

In *Shaky Pictures of Vanished Faces*, characters twist in the grip of forces beyond their understanding. Infused with the weird and uncanny, these stories probe the crannies and dead ends where humanity confronts the implacably alien, where even the most familiar faces begin to change, waver, and fade.

Lupus in Fabula
by Briar Ripley Page

Lupus In Fabula collects thirteen stories about the interplay of lust, violence, yearning, and grief; about becoming a monster and loving monsters; about transformation; about strange occurrences in sad, mundane lives. Whether you prefer witches and werewolves, grisly body horror, or surreal scenes of small town decay, this collection offers something to sink your fangs into.

The Nightmare Box and Other Stories
by Cynthia Gómez

A young queer man finds love at a magical clothing shop—and the courage to stand up to the homophobic cops. A witch who makes custom nightmares wonders why all her victims are connected to the Black Panthers—and who she's really working for. A soon-to-be father encounters a mysterious hitchhiker who tries pulling him back to the days of his violent past. A brand-new vampire, freshly hired at the blood bank, delights in her heightened sexual desire and superhuman strength.

Cynthia Gómez's debut collection is a magic-soaked love letter to Oakland, brimming with feminist rage. Its twelve stories center ordinary people—Latine, queer, working class-as they wield supernatural powers against oppression, loneliness, and dread.

Why Didn't You Just Leave
edited by Julia Rios and Nadia Bulkin

It's the question asked of any story about a haunting: *why didn't you just leave?* But if accounts of people who have stayed in haunted houses are any indication … it's never that simple.

In this book, you'll find twenty-two all-new stories about the reasons people *don't* leave scary situations—parents who stay in haunted houses to protect their children, convicts who literally can't leave their prison, retail workers who need a paycheck even if it's from a haunted workplace, trauma survivors suffering from agoraphobia, and more.

Featuring Shauntae Ball, I.S. Belle, Die Booth, Max Booth III, Christa Carmen, Raquel Castro, Alberto Chimal, Gabe Converse, Lyndsey Croal, Victoria Dalpe, Alexis DuBon, Corey Farrenkopf, Cassandra Khaw, Joe Koch, E.M. Linden, Steve Loiaconi, R. Diego Martinez, J.A.W. McCarthy, Suzan Palumbo, Tonia Ransom, Rhiannon Rasmussen, and Eden Royce. With illustrations by Luke Spooner, Yves Tourigny, and Yornelys Zambrano.

No Trouble at All
edited by Alexis DuBon and Eric Raglin

Politeness is the glue that holds society together. We are all expected to do our part—a pressure ripe with horror. Rotten, even. Whether we adhere to this contract or defy it, there are consequences. These fifteen stories respond to promises made for us, promises of compliance that cost too much to keep. Featuring Nadia Bulkin, Shenoa Carroll-Bradd, Ariel Marken Jack, Gwendolyn Kiste, Avra Margariti, J.A.W. McCarthy, R.L Meza, Marisca Pichette, J. Rohr, Simone le Roux, Angela Sylvaine, Nadine Aurora Tabing, Sara Tantlinger, D. Matthew Urban, and Gordon B. White.

Bitter Apples
edited by Eric Raglin

Cursed Morsels Press presents tales of teacher horror from Corey Farrenkopf, Emma E. Murray, Cynthia Gómez, Christi Nogle, D. Matthew Urban, Eric Raglin, and Aurelius Raines II. These writers have worked in the profession, and while their stories are fictional, the darkness they explore is all too real.

In *Bitter Apples*, you'll find students' ghosts haunting classrooms, desperate teachers joining cults, zombies plaguing underfunded schools, and more. The institution of education is rotting. How will we survive its horrors?

Shredded: A Sports and Fitness Body Horror Anthology
edited by Eric Raglin

Reader beware! This sports and fitness body horror anthology is dangerous. Side effects include monstrous steroid transformation, concussion-induced madness, possession by jock ghost, death by yoga cult, and more. Read with caution!

Featuring seventeen reps of terror by Nikki R. Leigh, Tim Meyer, Brandon Applegate, Red Lagoe, Caias Ward, RW DeFaoite, Mae Murray, D. Matthew Urban, Charles Austin Muir, Joe Koch, Michael Tichy, Rien Gray, Robbie Burkhart, Eric Raglin, Matthew Pritt, Madeleine Sardina, Alexis DuBon, and J.A.W. McCarthy.

Antifa Splatterpunk
edited by Eric Raglin

Fascism didn't die in 1945. Its grave was only temporary. Rising again, this undead ideology shambles into the present, gathering power and spreading destruction wherever it goes.

This monster stalks the pages of *Antifa Splatterpunk*, in which sixteen horror writers explore fascism's many terrors: police wielding strange bioweapons against the public, white supremacists annihilating their enemies through dark magic, and TV personalities vilifying all who defy the rising fascist tide.

But these stories are resistance: Nazi-killing demons, Confederate-slaying witches, and everyday people punching fascists in the teeth. Among the gore is a glimmer of hope that one day this monster will return to its grave and never rise again.

www.ingramcontent.com/pod-product-compliance
Lightning Source LLC
Chambersburg PA
CBHW020148120726
47903CB00007B/2458